Bedroom Shoot-Out!

Clint awoke abruptly, and attributed it to that survival instinct that had kept him alive for so long. He had heard something without realizing that he had heard it, and now he lay still and listened intently.

And heard it again.

A scratchy sound, like metal against metal.

Someone was trying to unlock the door to the room without the use of a key.

He slid his legs off the bed without waking Althea and drew his gun from the holster on the bedpost. As he did so he heard the lock click and hurriedly pushed Althea from the bed to the floor.

The door slammed open, and a man's silhouette showed in the doorway. He fired his gun at the bed four times and then Clint fired once, striking the man squarely in the chest. The assailant staggered backward, into the hallway, and fell to the floor.

Also in THE GUNSMITH series

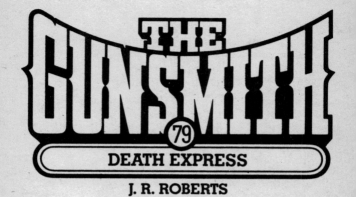

THE GUNSMITH

79

DEATH EXPRESS

J. R. ROBERTS

JOVE BOOKS, NEW YORK

THE GUNSMITH #79: DEATH EXPRESS

A Jove Book / published by arrangement with
the author

PRINTING HISTORY
Jove edition / July 1988

ISBN: 0-515-09649-0

Jove Books are published by The Berkley Publishing Group,
200 Madison Avenue, New York, New York, 10016.
The name ''Jove'' and the ''J'' logo
are trademarks belonging to Jove Publications, Inc.

PRINTED IN THE UNITED STATES OF AMERICA

10 9 8 7 6 5 4 3 2 1

ONE

The City of Kansas, Missouri, was situated right on the boundary between Missouri and Kansas. It was obviously growing in leaps and bounds, and would soon be a major city, such as Denver, Colorado, and Sacramento, California. It had a long way to go before it reached the level of New York or San Francisco, but Clint Adams felt that eventually it would get there.

In 1850 it had been called the Town of Kansas, and then in 1853 it became the City of Kansas. The railroad had arrived in 1865, and four years later the Hannibal Bridge was opened, the first structure to span the Missouri River.

All of these facts about the City of Kansas came to Clint's attention as a result of his dalliance with a lovely young lady named Kitty Flat—whose last name was grossly unearned, as she had as impressive a bosom as Clint had ever seen on a woman. Her breasts were large and rounded, with lovely, swollen undersides that fit neatly into his hands as he hefted them. At the same time he could thumb her russet-colored nipples, and she would moan and writhe, biting her lips and eventually climaxing just from the stimulation of her nipples. She was a remarkably sensuous woman,

1

but she was also very intelligent, and knew a lot about her home state and city. Of course, her job as a librarian gave her ample time to bone up on things that interested her.

Like Clint Adams.

They were having dinner together in the Kansas House dining room and she surprised him by producing a dime novel that had been written about him, out of New York.

"Where did you get that?" he asked, appalled.

"From the library, naturally," she said, fanning the pages. "It makes very interesting reading."

"Fiction."

"Perhaps, but surely it must be fiction based on fact, no?"

"No."

She frowned and said, "Are you angry with me?"

Kitty was all of twenty-four, with a sweet, innocent, pretty face that belied her sensuality and seemed out of place on so voluptuous a body. Still, it was a good face, with wide-set brown eyes, a straight nose, and a wide, not-too-full mouth that she used with deadly, wanton effectiveness.

"How could I be angry with you?"

"I didn't mean anything," she said, as if he had admitted that he *was* indeed angry with her. "I found it quite by accident and thought it might help me get to know you better."

"Tell me something, Kitty," he said, putting his hand on her arm, "the man you read about in that . . . that piece of fiction, did he impress you?"

"Impress me?" she repeated, blinking her eyes rapidly. She looked like a child who had been asked a difficult question by her schoolteacher. "I don't know if he impressed me—"

"Did he interest you, then? Or frighten you?"

"Frighten—yes, I believe he did frighten me a little, *and* interest me."

"Do I seem anything at all like that man?"

"Oh, no, that was what I was thinking," she said. "You're nothing at all like this book says you are."

"No," he said, shaking his head with great patience, "that book is not about me, Kitty. It's a piece of fiction about a fictional man."

"I see," she said contritely. "I'm sorry I brought it up."

"That's all right. Let's finish our dinner and not talk about it anymore."

"All right," she said. She snatched the book off the table and secreted it back in her purse, then picked up her knife and fork to finish her dinner.

At that moment Clint looked away to survey the roomful of diners, and saw a man seated alone at a table near a wall. In the crowded dining room he was the only person sitting alone. Clint looked at the doorway then and saw three men who were apparently arguing with the head waiter. It looked as if they wanted a table, and the head waiter was trying to explain that there weren't any to be had.

"What's wrong?" Kitty asked, turning her head to look behind her.

"Maybe nothing," he said. He smiled at her and said, "I'm just nosy." He cut a piece of steak and forked it into his mouth, and his attention once again wandered to the entrance to the dining room.

". . . hell, you say," one of the men shouted. Some

of the diners heard him and turned to see what the disturbance was. "We want to eat and we ain't leaving without being served."

"Please, sir . . ." the head waiter said.

"What about that table over there?" the spokesman for the three asked. He was pointing at the man who was sitting alone. He was a well-dressed man in his late forties who seemed unaware of the trouble that was brewing.

"That table only has one man at it," the man said. "Make him move."

"I have nowhere to put him, sir—"

"Hell, he's got a whole table to himself. He should be done eating, by now."

"Sir, I can't ask him—"

"Hell, we'll ask him ourselves," the man said and pushed the waiter aside. His two friends followed him as they all advanced on the lone man.

"Hey, friend," the man shouted, stopping directly in front of the man. His two friends stayed just one step behind him. They were all fairly large men, certainly larger than the lone diner who looked up at them.

"Can I help you?"

"Yeah, we need this table. Me and my friends are hungry."

"I'm afraid there's not enough room here for all of us," the man said. "I'd be willing to share the table, but—"

"Hell, we don't want to share no table, we want you to give us the table."

"But I haven't finished my dinner, as you can see," the man said.

"You've eaten enough of it," the man said. "Give somebody else a chance."

The waiter came up to the table and started to say, "Please, gentlemen, if you could be a little quieter—"

The spokesman for the three ruffians suddenly backhanded the waiter across the mouth, causing the man to stagger back into someone else's table. The two women who were dining there gasped as the man tried to use their table to keep his balance. Alas, he failed, and he and the table went tumbling to the floor, along with two unfinished dinners.

"Wait here," Clint said to Kitty.

"Clint—"

"Now see here," the well-dressed diner said, but the other man reached out and took hold of him by the shirtfront, cutting off his words.

"Are you gonna give up this table, or do we have to take it?"

"Well, a table is certainly not something to fight over—"

"Or die for, right, pilgrim?"

"Let him loose," Clint said.

The other two men turned their heads to look at Clint, but the first man kept staring at the seated man, holding him tightly by the bunched shirt in his hand.

"Mind your own business, mister," one of the other men said. The third man simply nodded, as if to emphasize his colleague's remark.

"This is my business, friend," Clint said. "You're disturbing my dinner and this man's dinner."

"Please . . ." the smaller man said, "it's all right . . ."

"No, it's not all right," Clint said. "Turn him loose . . . now!"

One of the men gave Clint a hard look and said, "Mister, you just bought yourself a whole bunch of trouble."

TWO

From her vantage point, things did not look good to Kitty Flat. She watched, nervously wringing her hands, wondering why Clint Adams was making absolutely no move to draw his gun.

Finally, the tension in the room was shattered by a single word.

"Jace," the first man said.

That was all the instruction the other two men needed. They both went to draw their guns, and Clint swung his right fist and struck one of the men on the jaw. The blow staggered him back into his friend, who dropped his gun on impact.

"Shit," the first man said. He was still holding the lone diner's shirtfront in his left hand, and now his right hand began to move for his gun.

"Don't," the man he was holding said, and suddenly a derringer was pressed against the larger man's temple.

Behind him, his two friends were fighting for their balance, and Clint reached out and relieved the second man of his gun. The third man's gun was still on the floor.

Clint pointed the gun at the two men.

The head waiter came over and stammered, "Should I c–call the police?"

"That's up to your customer here," Clint said, indicating the man who was now half-standing, half-seated, holding his little gun to his assailant's head.

"What's your name?" he asked the assailant.

"Walters, Fred Walters," he replied. He was sweating profusely.

"Do you and your friends aim to walk out of here on your own, or do you want the police to help you?"

"Uh, we'll walk, we'll walk . . ." the man said.

"All right then," the smaller man said, taking his derringer away from the man's head, "walk."

The man straightened up and looked at his two colleagues, who were under the gun in Clint's hand.

"Move!" Clint said.

"My gun," the second man said, indicating the gun in Clint's hand.

"Buy another one."

"Hey—"

Clint cocked the gun and said, "Move."

The third man began to bend over to retrieve his gun when Clint stopped him.

"Don't."

"It's my gun!"

"Not anymore."

The man frowned, but straightened up and started for the door. As the first man started past him Clint pulled the gun from his holster.

"Hey—"

"You're lucky you're alive, mister," Clint said. "You want to push it?"

The man stared at Clint's eyes, then shook his head and followed his friends.

"Here," Clint said as the men disappeared. He handed the head waiter both guns. "You'd better pick that one up, too."

"What do I do with them?"

"Keep them."

The head waiter didn't know what do do, so he ended up trying to placate the two women whose meals had been dumped on the floor, while holding all three guns.

Clint looked at the man with the derringer, who pulled back his sleeve and replaced the gun in the gambler's rig he wore there.

"That was pretty slick," Clint said. "Why didn't you pull it earlier?"

The man said, "It's a two-shot, and there were three of them."

"Good point," Clint said. "Well, enjoy your dinner."

The man looked down at his half-eaten dinner and made a face.

"I've lost my appetite. My name is Forrest Evers."

"Clint Adams."

The two men shook hands.

"I'd be pleased to buy you and your lady friend a drink, Mr. Adams. You did me a service here."

"It wasn't much," Clint said, "but I rarely turn down the offer of a drink."

"In the saloon, then? In an hour?"

"Sure, but the lady will have retired by then."

"Just us men, then."

"I'll be there. Thanks."

"Thank you."

Clint went back to his table, where he found Kitty staring at him.

"What's wrong?"

"You could have been killed."

"Not likely."

"But you took on two men with guns and never pulled your own."

"It wasn't necessary. Besides, someone might have gotten killed."

"Yes, you!"

"Like I said, not likely."

"You are like the man in the novels, aren't you?"

"Novels?"

Sheepishly, Kitty removed four dime novels from her bag, all purporting to be about "The Gunsmith, the Fastest Gun in the West!"

"Good Lord," Clint said, covering his eyes.

THREE

It was more like forty minutes when Clint entered the Kansas House Saloon, but Forrest Evers was there, propped up at the bar with a beer in front of him. Clint had given Kitty the key to his room, and she had gone upstairs to "ready herself" for him. At twenty-four she was still wonderfully, marvelously naive in many ways. She could never make love with Clint unless she'd had a bath first, and she was going to use the tub in his room and be ready for him when he arrived. (The Kansas House was one of the more progressive hotels in that they had installed bathtubs in their more ostentatious rooms, and Clint had decided to treat himself to one of these rooms. Those comforts had not quite reached west of Missouri yet.)

Clint went up to the bar and was noticed through the mirror by Evers.

"Mr. Adams," the man said, turning to face him. "Glad you could make it."

"The lure of a free drink is powerful stuff."

"To be sure. A whiskey?"

"Beer will be fine," Clint said, looking at the one the man himself was holding.

"Bartender, a beer for my new friend."

11

When the bartender brought the beer, Evers said, "Why don't we take a table and get better acquainted."

"Why not," Clint agreed.

The saloon was rather busy, but they were able to find a table toward the back of the room.

"I hope no one tries to take this one from us," Clint commented.

Evers laughed.

"If they do, I daresay we could repel them, you and I, eh?"

"I'm sure," Clint said.

Close-up the man looked younger than Clint had first thought, perhaps in his early forties. His clothing was certainly of an expensive cut, though, and he wore a diamond pinky ring on his left hand.

"That's not the kind of jewelry you should be wearing out West," Clint said.

"Ah, you have gleaned that I am an Easterner, eh?"

"It wasn't hard, but that sleeve gun is not an Easterner's move."

"You flatter me," Evers said. "No, that is a trick I learned from my brother, who is also not from the West. However, he now makes his living as a gambler in the West. He gave it to me and showed me how to use it."

"What's your brother's name?"

"Carleton Evers, although he goes by the name Carl. Why do you ask?"

"I've heard of him."

"Have you really?"

The man seemed delighted, and indeed, Clint had heard of Carl Evers. The man had a modest, yet somewhat impressive reputation as a gambler.

"I had no idea I was related to a celebrity."

"Now you know."

"Indeed. A toast, then, to my celebrated brother."

Evers downed his beer and then signaled a passing saloon girl for another. Clint noticed a fine line of veins in the man's nose, and wondered how long it would be before the man changed to what was obviously his regular drink, whiskey.

"I notice you did not say whether or not you approve of my gambler brother," Evers said, but then added quickly, "but that is neither here nor there. You showed yourself a gentleman by drinking the toast with me, whether you like him or not."

"I don't know him, Mr. Evers, I just know of him."

"Please, call me Forrest."

"All right. You can call me Clint. Tell me, Forrest, what do you do?"

"Well, Clint, I'm with the railroad. I had some business to conduct along our line out here and took the opportunity to drop in on my brother."

"What do you do for the railroad?"

"I built it."

"Really?"

"Oh, yes," Evers said, "how else do you think I can afford trinkets such as this?" He held up his hand and wiggled his fingers so that the pinky winked in the light.

Clint put his hand out and pushed Evers' hand down until it was flat on the table.

"Don't wave that around."

"Why not? If someone tries to take it, I have my little friend."

Clint realized now that the man had either started

with whiskey and turned to beer, or he'd consumed a lot of beers in forty minutes. He was on his way to being royally drunk.

"You won't always have the warning you need to produce that little peashooter."

The girl came with the beer and Evers paid her, frowning. When the girl left, he nodded and said, "You're probably right, Clint."

"You should leave it in your room."

"That won't be necessary. I'm leaving for Chicago in the morning."

"Is that where you live?"

"Yes. Chicago is my home — say, I have an idea."

"What?"

"We're launching a new rail line that will take passengers from Chicago clear to Denver. We're making a big fuss about it, inviting politicians, stars of the stage, bankers, all sorts of wealthy people. Many of them will be getting their first look at the Plains States. Why don't you come along as my guest?"

"I appreciate the invitation, but I don't anticipate being in Chicago—"

"Nonsense, nonsense, I owe you this. Your passage to Chicago to be paid in full. You will come as my guest, and accompany me on this historic trip. I insist! I insist!"

The man seemed adamant on paying Clint back in this way, and Clint was a bit intrigued by the notion of riding a train from Chicago to Denver.

"When is this trip supposed to take place?"

"Two weeks' time. The third of October. Will you come?"

"Well . . . I'll certainly think about it."

"Come a day or two early, and I'll show you Chicago," the man said, proffering his business card. On the back he had written his home address. Clint accepted the card and tucked it into his pocket.

"Now," the man said, "how about that whiskey?"

"Well," Clint said, "maybe just one."

FOUR

When Clint returned to his room Kitty was snug and warm under the covers in his bed. From her deep, even breathing he could tell she was asleep. The "one" drink with Evers had turned into—well, more than one, and the poor girl had tired of waiting for him.

He undressed and slid into bed with her. Her skin was very warm as he pressed his flaccid penis against her smooth, firm butt. Instantly, it began to harden, and she moaned and pushed herself back against him.

"Is that you?"

"No," he said, "it's the head waiter."

"Well, just let me roll over. My man didn't show up so you'll have to do."

She rolled over and their mutual aim was unerring despite the darkness. Their mouths came together and their tongues intertwined. They shifted their legs so that one of hers was between his, and the other atop him. He could feel her harsh pubic hair pressing against his swollen penis as she moved her hips back and forth.

"Mmm," she said, after the kiss had ended, "it is you."

17

"Disappointed?"

"Well, that head waiter was sort of cute—"

He slid a hand over her buttocks and squeezed one tightly.

"Ouch, all right, all right, I'm not disappointed."

He removed his hand.

"Not totally."

He slid his hand back down.

"It's up to you to see to it that I'm not disappointed," she said quickly.

"Well," he said, moving his hand so that he could probe her vagina from behind, between her thighs, "let me see what I can do about that."

"Mmm," she moaned as he found her clitoris.

The position was too involved, so he pushed her onto her back, tossed the covers away, and began to suck her nipples, once again pressing his finger to her clit from the front.

She groaned aloud as his finger rubbed her clit and his tongue flicked at her nipples. She reached down and took hold of his hard penis, wrapping her hand around it close to the base. Slowly, she began to pump him, moving her hand up and down the length of him, slowly at first, and then progressively faster.

Clint ran his tongue over the "V" between her breasts, and then started to move downward. As he shifted on the bed she released him reluctantly. He ran his mouth over her navel, poking it gently with his tongue, and then continued down over her wiry pubic hair until he reached his ultimate destination.

She was moist and ready and he tasted her in slow, sensuous lapping motions of his tongue. When he reached her clit she gasped and lifted her hips, brought her hands down to cup the back of his head.

"Oh, Clint, Jesus, lick me, mmm, yes, that's it, that's it . . . Jesus, that's it!"

When her orgasm started she stiffened and then suddenly began bouncing her bottom on the bed. She had told him one night that when he did that and she came, it was almost more than she could bear.

"Almost more," she added, making her point.

"Oooh, Lordy," she said, and it was what she always said when her orgasm was abating. It was his signal to mount her and drive his penis home.

Now she said, "Oh, Lordy!" in an entirely different tone of voice. She grabbed his buttocks and dug her nails into him while he proceeded to plunge into her. "Yes, yes!" she cried. He knew she liked it hard when she was on the bottom, long and slow when she was on top. He had never known a woman before with so many different likes and dislikes when it came to sex, but he wasn't complaining. He'd known too many women who liked it only one way, and that got boring after a while, no matter who the woman was.

When she began to grunt every time he drove into her, he knew she was approaching her next orgasm. She ran her hands up and down his sides, every so often scratching him with a sharp nail. He knew that while he was seeing Kitty he'd never be able to see another woman, because Kitty invariably marked him when they had sex. Nothing major, but a mark just the same. This time he figured he'd find scratches on his ribs *and* his ass.

Her vocalizing enabled him to time his own release to coincide with hers, and they both went over the edge together . . .

Clint had told Kitty that he was meeting Evers in the bar, and while they lay side by side, catching their breath, she asked him what they had talked about.

"He invited me to Chicago?"

"Have you ever been to Chicago?"

"No."

"Neither have I. I understand it's a very exciting place."

"Most big cities are."

"What big cities have you been to?"

"New York, San Francisco, Denver . . ." he said, naming a couple of others, as well.

"I've never been anyplace."

Clint wondered if she was pushing for an invitation to accompany him, when he hadn't even said whether or not he was going yet.

"Are you going?"

"I haven't decided."

"Why wouldn't you?"

Indeed, why wouldn't he? The invitation had come too readily—or was he just being suspicious? Perhaps Evers was simply extending the invitation out of honest gratitude.

He became aware that Kitty had asked him something else.

"I'm sorry, what?"

"I said, what is he inviting you to? Some kind of a party?"

"I guess you could call it that."

Against his better judgment he explained the situation to her, and he would later remember that he did.

"Sounds like fun," she said.

"I guess. There are other things to do for fun besides riding in a train for hundreds and hundreds of miles."

''Name one?'' she asked, but before he could, she snaked her hand down over his flat belly to his semierect penis and took hold of it.

"My thoughts exactly," he said.

FIVE

Chicago, Ill.
2 weeks later

The naked girl on the bed was a genuine beauty.

Her name was Lola Dillon, although there were times when she called herself Lulu DeLong, Lois Dilon, or—her *favorite nom de plume*—Lisa DeChance.

She was naked because it was her favorite state of being. Lying on her back, her full breasts barely flattened against her chest, which at thirty-one—a hard thirty-one, she admitted—was quite a feat. Then again, only twenty-eight of those thirty-one years had been hard, because it had been three years ago when she hooked up with Richard Sawyer.

The rest of her body was just as firm and lovely, because Lola—whose real name, though she never used it anymore, was Lily Mae Dennis—took very, very good care of herself.

Richard was the man in the room with her, and he was also naked, although he was not on the bed at the moment. He was standing with his back to her, smoking a long, thin cigar, looking out the window of their hotel room at Michigan Avenue.

He was thirty-three, tall and well built, with a trim

23

waist and the nicest ass she'd ever seen on a man. It was tight and smooth, and she loved to fondle it when he was inside of her. He had dark, curly hair that covered most of his body—his head, naturally, and then his chest, arms, and legs—but there wasn't a hair on that wonderful ass. More than once she'd likened the feel of his buttocks to that of a cue ball.

The man's full name was Richard Sawyer, of the Denver Sawyers. That is, the Sawyer family that had more money than any family in Denver, or in all of Colorado.

Why he stole for a living was beyond her, even though she had been with him for three years now.

At the moment, he was using the name Dick Dillon, as they were registered as husband and wife.

"Are you going to stare out that window forever, Richard?" she asked.

"Just a little longer, love," he replied without turning.

"I ache for you," she said, putting her hands over her breasts so she could rub the nipples with the flat palms of her hands. They were already distended, as she had been anticipating going to bed with him for the past hour. When they entered the room they had both undressed, but when she had gone to the bed, he had gone to the window.

He was thinking.

Sometimes she wished that he wasn't so smart.

Sometimes she wished that he weren't always thinking.

Even when they made love she knew he was thinking.

Sometimes she wished he'd just give her a good, long, mindless fuck!

She propped herself up on one elbow and contented herself with looking at his strong, broad back; his slim waist; his tight ass; and his long, muscular legs.

Why he wanted to rob a train was a mystery to her, but then his motivation for most of the things he did was beyond her—including why he'd picked her up from the street three years ago.

Richard Sawyer was thinking about the train.

In the breast pocket of his jacket was his invitation to ride on the trip from Chicago to Denver on the Central Pacific Railroad, and that was what had first given him the idea of robbing the train. There were supposed to be countless dignitaries aboard, rich men and women from every walk of life and—Jesus Christ!—they'd invited him to go along! What better alibi was there?

He drew on his cigar, enjoying the way the smoke slid smoothly down into his lungs. He knew he was standing buck naked in front of a window on the third floor of a hotel on one of the busiest streets in Chicago, and that he could clearly be seen from the street should anyone bother to look, but he didn't care. He knew how attractive he was to women, and he knew that most men eyed him with envy, so let them look. He had too much on his mind to worry about people seeing him naked.

The train was leaving in a week, and he had not yet chosen his "team." Lola/Lulu/Lily Mae was, of course, the first member of the team. When he had found her she was a common streetwalker, but he had seen through that to the woman *beneath* the whore, and she had evolved into one of the finest con women he'd ever had the pleasure to work with. She was also fabulous in bed. That was the one positive part of her former profession. She had learned every trick a woman could use on a man, some of which made him feel as if she were turning him inside out.

Thinking about it, his penis throbbed and began to thicken, but there were still things that had to be thought out . . .

He needed four or five others, probably all men. He knew he could get three of them from Chicago, but he had sent telegrams out for the other two, and had not yet heard back. Time was getting short, but he hoped he would not have to draft two inferior types to fill out the team. That would put the whole caper in jeopardy.

"Richard . . ." Lola said plaintively from behind him. For the purposes of this job, he preferred to call her *and* think of her as Lola.

He smiled and reached down to take his huge penis into his right hand. Idly rubbing, bringing it to life, he thought about Lola. He had never known an ex-whore who enjoyed sex so much, but of course he had to take some of the credit for that. He never knew a woman who could match him sexually, although Lola certainly came the closest.

His penis was standing almost at full mast now and he wondered if anyone was looking up from the street below. His penis was so large that he was able to lean a good portion of it against the window, enjoying the coldness of the glass.

"If any women see you, Dick, we're going to have a big crowd up here."

He laughed to himself. The little whore knew the right things to say. He was a vain man and knew it, and he knew that she occasionally played on that vanity to get her way.

Like now.

He put the cigar out on the windowsill and left it there, and turned to face her. He could see the hungry look on her face as she saw his penis, and he reached down to fondle his own balls, which were huge.

"Come on, little whore," he said to her, "come and get it."

In a split second she was on the floor before him, his penis in her mouth as she sucked at it greedily, hungrily. Slowly, he turned so that she was sucking him right in front of the window.

He was sorry they weren't on a lower floor, because a lot of women were missing a good show.

SIX

Allan Pinkerton sat behind his desk, puffing on a huge cigar. If his doctor saw him or worse, his son, William, they'd give him hell, but that was why he'd locked his door and opened the window.

Pinkerton had recovered very, very slowly from a recent illness, but he felt he was once again able to take control of the reins of his own detective agency.

Drawing on the cigar with savage pleasure his thoughts were to the current thorns in his side—the James boys and the Molly Maguires—both of whom were occupying much of his manpower. Now this damn railroad wanted detectives to ride their Denver-to-Chicago party train to protect their rich passengers from would-be robbers.

Where the hell was he supposed to get the extra men for that?

He rose from behind his desk, walked to the open window, tossed the cigar outside, and closed the window behind it. He fanned the air about his desk, and then went and unlocked his door.

"Can I help you, Mr. Pinkerton?" his secretary asked.

"Yes, I'd like to see my son, please."

"Yes, sir. I'll send a message."

He backed into his office and closed the door without so much as a "Thank you."

He sat back down behind his desk, again fanning the air to dispel the telltale smoke.

The railroad pest, Forrest Evers, had demanded detectives for his train, and he would get them.

Between him and his son they'd pick out two men they could do without, and give them a ride on a train.

Railroad poofs!

SEVEN

Clint Adams enjoyed the feel of Chicago. There were not many cities that felt quite like it, except perhaps New York City and San Francisco. Of course, he'd never been to Europe, so he didn't know how New York and Chicago and San Francisco would stand up to London or Paris. Maybe someday he'd get over there to do a comparison.

His hotel—The DuPont—was on Michigan Avenue, and he'd chosen it because Forrest Evers' office—the office of the Central Pacific Railroad—was also on that street, although—as it turned out—still quite some distance away.

The hotel had every convenience available to man, including the highest-class whores working the bar and restaurant. As pretty and classy as they were, Clint fended them off, although not easily. They were persistent and, of course, quite beautiful. Clint Adams, after all these years, had still never paid for a woman—no matter how beautiful and skillful she might have been—and he never would.

Upon arriving in Chicago, Clint purposely waited a couple of days before presenting himself at Evers' office, wanting, instead, to see what he could find

31

out about the man. From word of mouth—i.e., eavesdropping in some of the better bars and restaurants around town—and from some reading he did in the library, he found out that Forrest Evers was indeed an officer of the railroad, although he did have several partners. To say the least, the partners—and there were four of them—did not always get along, and Clint wondered how the other three would feel about Evers' having invited him along with all the other high-class guests. Then again, the other partners would no doubt have some guests of their own.

As Clint waited in Evers' outer office while the secretary announced him, he wondered if any of the high-class ladies working his hotel would show up on the train. Then he wondered if Evers' secretary would be there. A tall, full-breasted brunette, she certainly matched up well against the classiest ladies working the DuPont.

When Clint had first entered the office, the woman had studied him with cool, aloof detachment. It made him feel—even in his finest suit of clothes—like he was a bum who had wandered in off the street. Maybe she regarded everyone that way until it was proven otherwise.

"Yes?" she said.

"I'd like to see Mr. Evers."

"Is he expecting you?"

"I hope he is. He invited me here."

"I see," she said, doubt showing plainly on her lovely face. "And what is your name?"

"Clint Adams."

If she recognized it, she didn't allow it to show on her face.

"Please wait while I announce you."

That made Clint figure that she had recognized his name, otherwise she wouldn't be announcing him, but asking him what his business was.

He'd watched with great interest as she walked away from him through an impressive oak door, and was now waiting for her to reappear. She had a lot of things he liked in a woman. She was mature—probably in her early thirties—she was self-assured, she would obviously be experienced—in many things—and to top it off—by no means the most important thing—she was a tall, full-bodied beauty.

She came out a few minutes later and gave him something considerably warmer than the cool, appraising stare she'd greeted him with—namely, a smile.

"I'm sorry to have kept you waiting, Mr. Adams."

Obviously he was far from being a bum just in off the street, and she now knew that for sure.

"That's all right, Miss—"

"Saunders, Althea Saunders. I am Mr. Evers' assistant."

"I see."

"Would you come with me, please?"

"Sure, but shouldn't we tell your boss that we're leaving?"

She gave him another smile and said, "I am taking you to see Mr. Evers."

"Oh. Well, my loss. Lead on."

She turned and walked toward the oak door again and beyond, into Forrest Evers' office.

"Clint!" Evers greeted him warmly, rising from behind his desk with his hand extended. "I'm so glad you decided to come."

"As it turns out," Clint said, looking at Althea Saunders, "so am I."

Althea Saunders lowered her lashes demurely for a moment, then said to Evers, "If there's nothing else, sir?"

"But there is. Coffee?"

"Sure," Clint said.

"Coffee, Althea. How do you take it?"

"Black," Clint said, "just black, and strong."

"Althea?"

"I'll see to it, sir."

After she walked out, Evers wiggled his eyebrows at Clint.

"All that 'sir' stuff is for your benefit."

"I see," Clint said, although he didn't really. Was Evers saying that his relationship with Althea Saunders was more than businesslike, or that she simply addressed him less formally when they were alone?

"She doesn't look like the type to make coffee for her boss."

"Make it? Lord, she doesn't make it," Evers said, rolling his eyes. "She made that damn clear when I hired her. No, she'll have it brought in from outside. Don't worry, though, it'll be good. It comes from a little place across the street. Their food is awful, but they make damn good coffee."

"That's good," Clint said, for want of something else to say. He wasn't at all sure that he was glad he had come.

"Sit down, sit down. Damn, I'm glad you came. You won't regret it."

"I hope not," Clint said. He sat in a well-padded chair in front of Evers' desk, while Evers lowered himself into a leather swivel chair.

"When does the train leave?" Clint asked.

"The end of the week, Saturday. What hotel are you staying at?"

"The DuPont."

"Nice, but a little long in the teeth. I can have you moved to the Elmont Plaza, over on—"

"I like the DuPont," Clint said.

"Fine," Evers said, without missing a beat, "I'll have your bill taken care of."

"That's not necessary, Mr. Evers—"

"Hey, I thought we were done with all that 'Mister' stuff," Evers said. "Old drinking companions like us don't stand on formality."

"Forrest, then. I'm perfectly able to handle my own hotel bill."

"As you wish, but you are taking me up on the free trip to Denver, right?"

"Yes, I am."

"Good, very good. Well, I have your ticket right here," Evers said. He opened his top drawer and took out a long white envelope. He extended it across the desk and Clint accepted it.

"There are also instructions in there on how to get to the depot to board."

"That'll come in handy," Clint said, tucking the ticket away in his jacket. Although he had dressed quite differently than he normally did—a dark suit and his shiny black boots—he was still wearing his gun on his hip. To go without it would have made him feel naked.

As Clint rose, Evers said, "Hey, where are you going?"

"I thought I'd take a little stroll around your city."

"Clint, I could show you around myself."

"You're busy, Forrest. I don't want to take you away from your work."

"Well, hell, Althea's bringing coffee."

"Tell her I'm sorry I couldn't wait," Clint said apologetically. He started for the door.

"I could have her show you around."

Clint stopped with his hand on the doorknob, then turned back to face Evers.

"You know," he said, "I think I will wait for that coffee, after all."

EIGHT

After Clint Adams left with Althea Saunders, the connecting door between Forrest Evers' office and that of his partner—one of his partners—Sam Grain, opened, and Grain stepped in.

A tall, well-proportioned man most of his life, Grain was now fifty-one, and he had started to thicken around the middle. He had close-cropped gray hair, and was given to wearing garish vests with his dark, solid-colored suits.

"Was that Adams?" he asked.

"It was."

"You gonna have Althea fuck his brains out?"

Evers frowned.

"That would be up to her, wouldn't it, Sam?"

"Oh, I forgot," Grain said. "You don't like words like that."

Evers did not rise to the bait. Of his three partners, Sam Grain was his least favorite and—almost as some sort of punishment on earth—Grain was the partner he dealt with most of all. The other two, Ted Covington and Albert Small, mostly supplied money and connections, while Grain and Evers did most of the hustling.

"Did he take the job?"

"I didn't offer him a job."

"You said you could get the Gunsmith for security on the train—"

"And I have," Evers said. "He'll be coming along as my guest."

"Will he be bringing his gun?"

"Sam," Evers said, "the man always wears his gun. He'd be a walking target without it. He probably wears the damn thing to bed."

"We could ask Althea about that later on, couldn't we, Forrest?"

Again, Evers refused to be drawn into an argument with Grain. Needling Evers seemed to be Grain's sole joy in life.

"Well, as long as he's along. What about the Pinkertons?"

"I'll be talking with William Pinkerton later today," Evers said.

"William? Why not Allan?"

"Apparently Allan Pinkerton is still not at his best. William will do fine, Sam. In fact, it will be better if I talk to him. At least we get along."

"Well, let me know what happens at that meeting, will you?"

"Why don't you come along?" Evers hated when Grain skipped meetings, because it made him feel like a lackey to have to report the proceedings to him each time. He could have sworn that Grain didn't attend meetings specifically for that reason.

"I have to talk to the senator."

"Creighton?"

"Yes. Apparently, he'd like to have some female companionship on the cruise."

Evers' face turned red.

"I don't want any whores on this train!" he said forcefully.

"Relax, Forrest. You act like whores are dirty or something."

"Dirty? Why they're—"

"Don't worry, I'll get the senator his woman. You won't have to be involved with that at all."

Abruptly Grain walked to the connecting door, passed through it, and closed it softly behind him. That was something else Evers disliked about Grain. The man never said "good-bye" or "that's all" or anything. He simply finished a sentence and, while it hung there, left the room.

Evers sat for a moment, trying to remember why he and Grain had become partners. Each time he tried to recall the reasons it got harder and harder.

NINE

William Pinkerton sat across from his father, who was seated behind *his* desk. He wished his father would either go home or back to the Denver office.

Then again, his father's knowledge of the Denver office and its operatives had solved the problem created by Forrest Evers and his railroad.

"So you've picked out the operative we'll send on the trip to Denver?" William asked. He was a tall, dark-haired man in his early forties who, no matter how hard he tried, couldn't shake the brand "Old Allan's boy."

"I have."

"Who is he?"

"He's a she."

"A woman?"

"Very good, Bill," Allan Pinkerton said to his son. "You picked up on that right away."

William Pinkerton closed his eyes for a moment, and then opened them, but his father was still there, looking as white-haired and superior as always, albeit somewhat pale and drawn from his recent illness.

"Who is she?"

"Ellie Lennox."

"Do I know her?"

"No, but she's here."

"In Chicago?"

"Yes. I transferred her here last year."

"She's been working here for a year?"

"That's right."

"What's her name again?" William asked.

"Lennox, Ellie Lennox."

For the life of him, William couldn't conjure up the face that went with the name.

"What has she been doing? Office work?"

"Field work."

"A woman?"

"We have several women working in the field, Bill."

"In Denver, maybe," William said, "but not in Chicago."

"I'm having a meeting this afternoon with Evers," Allan said. "Miss Lennox will be here. I suggest you be here, as well, and you can meet her."

"I wouldn't miss it."

"Be here at four, then. Is there anything else I should know about?"

"Just one thing."

"What?"

"The Gunsmith is in Chicago."

"Clint Adams?"

Bill toyed with the idea of saying, "Very good, Father, you picked up on that right away," but decided against it.

"Yes."

"What is he doing here?" Allan's dislike of Adams came across quite plainly—or plaintively—in his voice.

"We don't know."

"Well, find out. Where is he staying?"

"At the DuPont."

"I want to know why he's here, Bill," Allan said, "and I want to know by this afternoon. Understood?"

"Understood."

"Well, get to it!"

William Pinkerton just barely caught himself before saying, "Yes, sir."

God, he hated when his father did that to him.

Allan Pinkerton admitted that his intense dislike of Clint Adams was unreasonable. He disliked Adams for the same reason he disliked Talbot Roper. Roper had once been Pinkerton's top operative, until their personalities dictated a parting of the ways. Roper now had his own detective agency.

Likewise, it was a clash of personalities that kept Pinkerton and Adams from liking each other, and yet there was a mutual respect there, albeit grudging. On more than one occasion Pinkerton had offered Adams a position with the Pinkertons, and Adams had always turned him down. It was just as well, he thought, as they wouldn't have lasted long working together.

Adams and Roper, now that would be a pair. If they ever decided to work together, they might give even the Pinkertons a run for their money.

Allan Pinkerton wanted to know exactly what Adams was doing in Chicago, and he wanted to know quickly.

TEN

Ellie Lennox was nervous.

Ellie had long, dark hair. She was five-four with big brown eyes, a wide mouth, and full, firm breasts. She was not a beauty, but she was very pretty, and she knew it.

In point of fact, at one time not long ago she hadn't even known that for sure, until Clint Adams showed her. Knowing Clint Adams had changed her outlook on her life, both her social and business life.[1] There had been some men since Clint, but no one special. There had been some interesting assignments for a while after Clint had left Denver, but then Old Allan suddenly had her transferred to Chicago, and any progress she might have been making had come to a halt.

Clint had taught her that patience was as important as skill, so she had been waiting patiently ever since the transfer, and now maybe her patience was going to pay off. She had a three-thirty appointment with Allan Pinkerton in his son William's office. She had only seen William once or twice since her transfer,

1. THE GUNSMITH NO. 53: DENVER DUO

as she was reporting to and getting her assignments from Ray Whitman, William's executive assistant. She wondered if William would be there as well.

But what she was really wondering was if this was it, the big assignment she had been waiting for, where she could prove herself.

Pete Bateman didn't like trains, but he did like working with Richard Sawyer. Every time he worked a job with Rich, he ended up with a lot of money. Unfortunately, in between jobs, he lived high enough to go though all of the money he made, so whenever Rich Sawyer called, he came, even if it meant riding on a train—as unnatural an act as Pete Bateman could think of. The only way for a man to travel was on horseback.

Bateman was a tall, rangy man in his late thirties, good with his fists, his gun, and smart enough to know when to use one instead of the other. He was not, however, smart enough to keep himself from being almost always broke. Richard Sawyer, however, was that smart.

Pete Bateman was number three on Sawyer's team.

Lenny Germaine's real name was Leonard German, but even though he was known in the trade as "Lenny the German," he thought "Germaine" sounded classier.

Lenny the German was about five-five, slender, and pale-skinned, with very dark hair that he wore slicked down. The result, when he dressed properly, was a very compact, yet regal look, which Richard Sawyer told him was needed for this job.

Lenny liked to work with Sawyer for the same reason as Bateman, and consequently, he was the number four member of the team.

"Who is number five?" Lola asked Sawyer.

For once they were in their hotel room together, totally dressed. Sawyer was seated at a table with his handwritten notes spread in front of him. He planned every job he pulled carefully and precisely, putting it all down on paper first. All those notes only confused Lola.

"I know who I want," he said, looking up from his notes, "and I know who I'll use if I can't get my first choice."

"And who is your first choice?"

"Stennett."

Lola made a face, as if she had just bitten into the world's most sour-tasting lemon.

"I know, I know," Sawyer said, "you don't like him, but he's the best."

"And who's the second choice?"

"Kendall."

"He's strictly second-rate," she said. "You've said so yourself."

"I know, Lola, but he's here in Chicago."

"And Stennett?"

Sawyer shrugged.

"I sent some telegrams to try and locate him."

"And no reply?"

"The only reply will be if and when he shows up."

"There's only four days left."

"Four days before the train leaves," Sawyer said, "but I need three to go over every aspect of the plan.

No, if Stennett isn't here by tomorrow morning, it'll have to be Kendall."

Lola could tell by his tone of voice that he hoped he wouldn't have to use Kendall. For the sake of the success of the job, she hoped Stennett would arrive. She'd just have to forget how contemptible she found him and try to work with him, for Richard's sake.

"Okay, so that's five," Lola said. "Is that all we need?"

"No, we'll need some bodies, men who can carry guns, but that's no problem. My only problem is Stennett."

"We can do it without him."

"We can," Sawyer said, "but I'd prefer not to try. I'm no killer, Lola, you know that. There are things we need Stennett for."

Lola shivered, then put her hands on Sawyer's shoulders while he continued to look at his notes. She knew Sawyer respected Stennett, but what she didn't know was whether or not he was afraid of him.

In point of fact, Rich Sawyer didn't know that, himself.

ELEVEN

Tom Stennett arrived in Chicago late that afternoon, and took a room at one of the cheapest, most run-down hotels in town. In the morning, he'd go over to Rich Sawyer's hotel and listen to what Rich had to say. From past experience, he felt that he'd probably be working for Sawyer for the next few days or weeks. Sawyer's plans were usually that good.

Stennett—unlike Pete Bateman—knew how to save his money, and could have stayed at any expensive hotel he wanted, but he didn't feel that he fit in with the type of people he'd find there. The Fifth Street Hotel was more his style, and as he took his key from the clerk, he asked if there were any girls working the hotel.

"Oh, yessir. The finest in town."

Stennett knew that was a lie.

"I want a clean one," Stennett said, "preferably a blonde, and not too skinny. Also not too old. Can you handle that?"

"For the right incentive, sir, we can handle anything."

"What's the right incentive?"

The clerk named a price, and Stennett handed it

over. The clerk pocketed the money, looking very satisfied.

"She'll be upstairs within the hour, sir."

"Good. You got a bathtub?"

"In the back."

"Get me some hot water. I'll be back down in ten minutes."

"Yessir. That'll be half a dollar."

Stennett pinned the man with a hard stare and said, "Take it out of what I just gave you."

The clerk withered beneath the man's gaze and said, "Of course, sir, of course."

Stennett was not an attractive man. In fact, he might have been best described as ugly. For this reason he chose to use whores for his needs, rather than trying to overcome his ugliness with good manners or charm—neither of which was his to command. Stennett was a killer, and he looked and acted like a killer, and the clerk reacted to that look. Suddenly the man wondered if he hadn't overcharged the new guest.

No amount of money came in handy when you were dead.

Suddenly Stennett reached over and took hold of the clerk's shirtfront. The man just knew he was going to die. Maybe if he gave the money back . . .

"Just remember," Stennett said, "if I catch a disease from this girl, you'll catch a worse one—a fatal one. Make sure she's clean, and I don't mean that she's had a bath."

"Oh, yessir—I mean, no sir, she'll be clean. We don't use no diseased girls. It's bad for business, heh, heh . . ." the man babbled.

Stennett released the man, who silently gave thanks that he was still alive. As the guest went up to his room, the clerk turned to go and get his bath ready. As an afterthought, he turned back and looked at the name in the register. He read it a few times, mouthing it silently, then decided he didn't know it. The man called Tom Stennett may not have been famous enough for the clerk to recognize the name, but the clerk had recognized one thing. Fame or no, Stennett was a killer.

You don't get eyes like that in any other profession.

TWELVE

"Bill, this is Ellie Lennox," Allan Pinkerton said, introducing Ellie to his son William.

"I'm pleased to meet you, Mr. Pinkerton," she said to William.

"Miss Lennox," the younger Pinkerton said, "I've heard a lot about you."

She knew that was a lie. He didn't know her from a hole in the wall, and eighteen months ago she would have said that. Controlling her temper—and her sharp tongue—was something else she had learned from Clint Adams.

"I'm pleased to hear you say that."

The other person in the room was Ray Whitman, her immediate superior and William Pinkerton's executive assistant. He had been with the Pinkertons for almost twelve years, but privately Ellie doubted that the man had ever been in the field. He was in his forties, balding and short, and although she felt the way she did, she still could not have questioned his administrative talents.

"Miss Lennox, has Ray told you what we want you to do?" William asked.

"Yes, he has."

To say she was excited would have been an understatement. Her assignment was to head up the security staff of the Central Pacific Railroad's Chicago-to-Denver run. She'd read about this trip in the papers, and knew that dozens of famous people—politicians, actors, actresses, businessmen—were going to be on board.

"I'm honored to be asked to do this, sir."

"And well you should be," Williams said. "It's no small task."

"I realize that, sir."

"Are you up to it?"

"I am, sir."

"That's good. Ray," he said, giving Whitman his attention. "See to it that Miss Lennox gets all of the particulars, will you? We wouldn't want her to miss the train, would we?"

"No, sir, we wouldn't," Whitman said, sharing a laugh with his boss. "Come along, Ellie."

"Excuse me, sir," Ellie said to William Pinkerton.

"Yes?"

"Uh, how many people will I be commanding? I mean, how many will there—"

"Do you know Al Wyatt?"

"Yes." Al Wyatt was the company joke. Nobody knew how he became a Pinkerton, or how he stayed one.

"He's your security force."

"Just him and me?" she asked.

"That's right."

"Ellie—" Whitman said, warningly, but to no avail.

"You're joking," Ellie said to the three of them.

"I don't joke about business, Miss Lennox."

"But Al Wyatt? Aside from the fact that he's incompetent, to expect me to secure a trainload of people with just two people is—"

"Impossible?" Allan Pinkerton broke in.

She stopped and stared at him.

"Miss Lennox, are you telling us that it is impossible?"

"I—no, I—"

"Are you telling us you do not want this assignment?"

"I—no, I'm not saying that . . . at all."

"Then go with Mr. Whitman. He will apprise you of the rest of the particulars in this case. Thank you for coming."

"I—you're welcome . . . sir."

Whitman herded Ellie out of the room before she could author another outburst.

When they reached Whitman's office, Ellie Lennox exploded again.

"The old man's senile, and the younger one is just plain crazy!"

"That kind of talk is not going to get you anywhere in this agency, Ellie."

"Ray, what the hell is going on?"

A helpless look came over the man's face.

"I don't know, Ellie. The old man—well, he and railroad people don't get along. He thinks this business of dining cars and private cars on railroads is nonsense."

"He may be right, but if he's not really going to give them adequate security, why send anyone at all?"

Whitman shrugged and said, "Politics. At least he can say he sent someone."

"Yeah, me and . . . and Al Wyatt?"

"Ellie . . . just do the best you can."

"I'm being set up, Ray," she said. "If that train gets hit, I can't stop it with two people. I'll take the fall, not the Pinkertons."

"You're still working for us."

She shook her head furiously.

"He'll find some way to put the blame on me."

"Do you want to turn the assignment down?"

"No! I won't give him the satisfaction," she said. "I'll see this through to the end, Ray,—wherever and whatever that is. I'll see it through!"

"She's unstable," William said.

"She's got spunk," Allan said.

"I don't like spunk."

"She came in very handy in Denver . . . from time to time."

"Then why did you transfer her here?"

Allan Pinkerton smiled and said, "Because it's my agency and I can do as I please."

William Pinkerton did not need to be reminded of that.

"Now, what have you found out about Adams?"

"He's been in town several days, but went to see Forrest Evers this morning."

"Evers," Allan said, frowning. "Don't tell me he's involved in this train thing?"

"As near as we can figure, he's among the guests."

"With the caliber of people who are going to be on this train," Allan Pinkerton said, "why and how would Clint Adams fit in?"

"I . . . don't know."

"No, and neither do I," Allan said. "That bothers me, Bill. That really bothers me."

There was a moment of silence between them and

then Allan said, "Have someone talk to him."

"I'll do it myself."

"No," Allan said, "no, let Whitman do it."

"Ray's not a field man, Father. He never has been."

"He won't present any kind of a threat to Adams. Let Whitman do it. You'll give him his instructions."

"All right, Father. As you say."

"Right, then, let's have Mr. Forrest Evers brought in and tell him he's got his security."

THIRTEEN

Given the circumstances of their first meeting, the last place Clint expected to find Althea Saunders that evening was in his bed.

She had shown him some of the better sights of Chicago that afternoon, and then he had invited her to dinner, not really expecting her to accept.

She did.

After dinner, he had visions of her in his bed, but he expected her to have him take her directly home.

She didn't.

She had virtually invited herself to his room, and upon entering she turned into his arms for a first kiss. It was a gentle, testing touch of the lips at first, and then her mouth opened and her tongue slipped into his. Suddenly she was a different woman, clawing at his clothes and hers. They managed to undress each other with only the slightest interruptions of the kiss — to keep from falling off balance — and then moved to the bed together.

The moon was shining into the room and in its light he saw her crouch between his legs and take his penis into her mouth. She moaned as she sucked him, cupping his balls in one hand and holding his penis at its

59

base with the other. Her head bobbed up and down at an ever-increasing speed, until he was almost ready to come.

At that point, having brought him to full readiness, Althea Saunders had then proceeded to ride him long and hard, so that, at this moment, she was sitting astride him, with the full length of his rigid penis deep inside of her, and there was no resemblance to the cool, detached woman he'd met earlier that day.

Now she tossed her head back, exposing the long, lovely lines of her neck, and moaned aloud as her orgasm gripped her. At that same moment Clint found himself no longer able to control himself, and he began to fill her with long, hard spurts.

He had been right about one thing. She certainly was experienced.

"Well," he confessed later, "I never expected this."

"Why not?" she asked.

They were lying side by side with no bed covers, their bodies covered with a sheen of perspiration.

"I know," she said, before he could answer. "The Ice Princess, right?"

"It is the image you project," he admitted.

"I can't help it," she said. "I don't do it on purpose, that's just the way I . . . I am."

"Well, you're not that way now."

She turned her head to look at him. Her hair was loose and spread on the pillow around her head. She certainly was *not* the Ice Princess now.

"Well, we're in a different set of circumstances now," she said. "This is pleasure, not business."

"I should hope so."

"What do you mean by that?" she asked sharply.

"Nothing," he said. "I just meant that I hoped what we just did was pleasurable for both of us."

"Oh, it was," she answered, "it certainly was. In fact," she added, turning toward him. "I'd even be willing to do it again."

He put his hand on her hip and then slid it around to cup her left buttock.

"No," he said, teasingly, "really?"

"Yes," she said, sliding her leg up over him and licking the sweat from his shoulder, "really."

"Again?" he said.

"Again," she said, eyes shining.

And they did.

"So," Althea said later, stretching her hands up over her head, pulling that marvelous body taut, "tell me how you rate an invitation on this little junket."

He saw no reason not tell her about his first meeting with Forrest Evers.

"Forrest did that?" she asked. "With the sleeve gun, I mean?"

"He did."

She laughed.

"I wouldn't have thought he had it in him. I didn't know about his brother, either."

"Maybe that's not something you tell your . . . assistant about."

He watched her as he said it, waiting for her to react.

She did, by laughing again.

"Forrest is happily married, Clint. I'm his assistant, but that's all."

"And you don't make coffee."

"Secretaries make coffee," she said, "not assistants."

"I see," he said. "I'll remember that."

"Then Forrest didn't . . . hire you?"

"I don't hire out, Althea," he said. "Gunmen do that."

"But, I thought . . ."

"You thought what?"

"What I'd heard about you . . ." she said lamely.

"You can't always believe what you hear, Althea," Clint said. "Only what you see."

She looked properly chastised for a moment, then reached over and ran her hand over his penis, causing it to react immediately, beginning to swell.

"And," she added, "what you feel."

Althea Saunders was confused.

After leaving Clint Adams' room—weary in a warm, wonderful way—she was seized by guilt. She had only gone to bed with him because she had been ordered to. It was part of her job. That had been why she'd reacted so sharply when he made the remark about business and pleasure. If she was going to continue seeing him, she was going to have to be more careful about her reactions.

The confusion came into it because now that she had spent a half a day with him, and been to bed with him, she felt confused about where her allegiance should lie. Certainly he didn't deserve to be spied on, but she also didn't think that she deserved to be in jail, and if she refused to spy on him, that was where she would end up. She liked him a lot, and under normal circumstances would have been glad that they were both going to be on the train to Denver. These were not normal circumstances, however, and she didn't like him quite enough to go to jail.

Her present predicament was, by her own admission, her own fault. She had gotten herself into a situation where she could not deny her employer *anything*—and he often took advantage of that fact—as he no doubt would tonight.

At that moment she was on her way from Clint Adams' bed to his.

FOURTEEN

Sam Grain smoked his big, fat cigar with great satisfaction. The luckiest day of his life—well, one of them—was when he caught Althea Saunders—then an employee of his in the bookkeeping department of one of his companies—stealing from him. How else would he have gotten a woman like that to warm his bed? It never mattered to him that she was there unwillingly, it only mattered that she was there—as she would be, shortly.

Instead of turning her over to the police when he discovered her thievery, he made a deal with her. If she would work for him, not denying him anything, he would keep her out of jail. She had agreed.

The first thing he had done was take her to bed and degrade her in every way possible. She had done everything he asked her to do and had never complained. Apparently this woman felt that a deal was a deal—especially when a long jail sentence was the only alternative.

The second thing he had done was send her to Forrest Evers to look for a job, knowing full well that Evers needed an assistant. He had warned her of what would happen if she failed to get the job, and get it she did.

The railroad was just one of Grain's interests, and he felt he needed a spy in Evers' office to make sure that his best interests were served. In any partnership, he felt that a spy in the other's camp was essential, and often that had proved to be true.

Even before Althea had met Clint Adams, Grain had decreed that she would go to bed with him and find out what he knew and how loyal he was to Evers.

Grain drew long and hard on the cigar, and as he blew the last of his smoke rings, Althea's key fitted itself into the lock of his room. She entered and he could tell from the flushed look on her face that she'd had sex with Adams—and had probably enjoyed it. Damn her, she never had that look on her face after being bedded by him.

She stopped short, obviously startled by the fact that he was naked. His penis was standing long and hard, like a pole.

"Sam—"

"First get undressed," he said, crushing out the cigar.

"What? But—"

"Get undressed, Allie, and come to bed."

He wanted her while that flush was still on her face. He wanted to be able to pretend that he had put it there.

Dutifully, she removed her clothing. She hated when he called her "Allie." It implied a closeness which they did not enjoy.

Grain watched with pleasure—a pleasure that increased dangerously each time he did watch—as her clothing fell away, and as she moved naked to his bed. He looked at her for a few moments as she sat there. The dejected slump of her shoulders did nothing to mar the proud beauty of her breasts. They were full and round, marvelously firm, with large brown nipples. Except for those breasts, and a full, pear-shaped bottom, her body was slender and taut. He enjoyed looking at her, but even more than that he enjoyed using her.

He instructed her to get on all fours, doggie-style, and then took her from behind, brutally. When he came, he roared and bruised her flesh with his hands, then withdrew from her and pushed her aside. He did not look at her face immediately, for he knew what he would find there. Intense distaste, bordering on hatred.

Well, that was her problem. She had made her bed, and now she was lying in his.

"All right," Sam Grain said, "I've given you time to freshen up. What does he know?"

Althea stood before him, fresh from a bath, naked and utterly beautiful. Sometimes she cursed the day he caught her stealing, but there was no going back now. She was stuck with him and he with her. Love never occurred to him, but he knew that he never wanted to be without her, without the power to command her.

"Nothing."

"What do you mean, nothing?"

She propped her leg on a chair and leaned over to rub it with the towel. The move made her breasts dangle and sway as she moved.

"He's coming along as Forrest's invited guest, and nothing more."

"Surely Forrest expects more."

"He expects that having Clint on board will bolster security, but he has never actually asked Clint to *act* in a security capacity."

Grain thought about it, then laughed heartily, lighting another cigar.

"He's tricked the Gunsmith into coming along."

"Yes."

"But will he be able to trick him into helping?"

"He doesn't feel he has to. He's going to let it be known that the Gunsmith is on board. He feels that will deter anyone from trying anything."

"Forrest is a smart businessman, but when it comes to people, he's a fool."

"Choosing you as a partner should be proof of that."

Grain laughed again.

"I'll allow you that because you've had a long and difficult day."

More and more, Althea Saunders thought that those words—long and difficult—described her life, especially since she'd met Sam Grain.

"Why is he a fool?" she asked.

"Because there are people who would try to rob this train simply *because* the Gunsmith is on it."

"That's silly."

"But it's the way men are, my dear. Robbing this train, with the list of famous people who will be on board, would be a feather in any man's cap, but robbing it while the Gunsmith was aboard? That's a reputation-maker."

"So you're convinced that the train is going to be robbed?"

"I'm convinced someone will try. There's been enough publicity about this thing to assure that."

"And in spite of that, you're going along with it?"

"I'm not only going along with it, my dear," Grain said, "but I'm also going along for the ride. In fact," he said, with great satisfaction, "I wouldn't miss it for the world."

FIFTEEN

Clint Adams lay on his back with his hands behind his head, inhaling the scent that Althea Saunders had left on the sheets. It was a mixture of her sex, her sweat, and her very personal scent, the one that every person carried around with them.

He liked them all. In fact, he liked her.

That is, he wanted to like her, but he was suspicious of her. He'd had many encounters with women, and had even bedded some on a moment's acquaintance, but there was something about this particular encounter that didn't ring true.

He hoped he was wrong, but he was paying heed to his instincts, and he'd rarely gone wrong doing that.

Althea Saunders lay in bed next to Sam Grain, who was snoring. He had taken her again before going to sleep, and she wished that she could get up and take another bath. She also wished she had the nerve to kill him while he slept, but she knew that she could never do that.

Could she?

• • •

Forrest Evers was in bed at his home, lying next to his wife.

His meeting with the Pinkertons, both Allan and William, had left him dissatisfied. They had told him that he would have security, and that they would introduce him to the operative who would head up the security force, but what they would not tell him was how many men they were assigning.

Evers' concern was that Pinkerton would not give him enough men for adequate security. For that reason he was glad that Clint Adams would be aboard.

He felt badly about using Clint this way, but once the trip was over, he hoped to make it up to him.

The other thing on his mind was one of his partners, Sam Grain. This trip had been Evers' idea—borrowing, of course, the general idea of luxury cars from George Mortimer Pullman. Pullman had, of course, invented the luxury cars, with hinged upper berths and hinged seats and seatbacks that could be flattened for night travel. From there he had gone to sleeping cars and parlor cars, but Evers was going to go a step further. His cars were going to be the most magnificently upholsered travel cars, with expensive wall hangings, hand-carved paneling, and dining service . . .

The only problem with the whole setup was that the way it now stood, Grain would get as much credit as Evers, and Forrest Evers didn't intend for that to happen.

He had to get rid of Sam Grain, once and for all.

Richard Sawyer was on top of Lola Durant, his rigid penis buried deep inside of her. He was driving into her so hard that she grunted with every thrust, but she wasn't complaining. On the contrary, she loved it. He was always like this just before a job, like a rutting bull who couldn't get enough—and neither could she. She knew she'd enjoy these next few days, and that they would have to last her, because once the job started, there would be no sex. That was the way he was. On the train, and until the job was successfully pulled off, he would be celibate.

And he would expect her to be, also.

She hoped that this time she'd be able to. On the last job she'd had to pick out a young man—little more than a boy, really, just barely seventeen—and secretly bed him, her itch had become so unbearable.

Lola just was not the type to go without sex for very long.

To Sawyer it seemed as if his penis was becoming more and more engorged and yet refused to discharge. He knew that it would take a while before he finally came, because now they were starting the planning stage of the job. Lola grunted and moaned beneath him, but he knew that she was enjoying it. He also knew that, while he was celibate during a job, she had often sneaked off to have sex with someone. He didn't mind. He knew that the men—and, in some cases, the boys—that she'd had meant nothing to her. She just couldn't be without sex for very long. Knowing that about her, he didn't fault her for looking for it somewhere else when he couldn't give it to her.

He couldn't afford to let it bother him. His concentration had to be completely on the job. In the morning the rest of their team would arrive, and hopefully Stennett would be among them. If he was, then Sawyer's mind would be free of any worry, and he'd be able to concentrate fully on the job at hand.

If Stennett wasn't there—well, there was a point during every job that involved a group of people when the people had to be shown you meant business. That invariably meant hurting someone or, in some cases, killing someone.

Stennett was invaluable, that way. He had no conscience, and was ready to kill at a moment's notice.

Without Stennett, that job would fall to someone less reliable—and maybe even Sawyer, himself.

He hoped like hell Stennett would show up. If Sawyer had to kill someone himself—

—but his thoughts were interrupted by Lola, who was screaming as if someone were killing *her,* and then he was coming, and everything but that moment faded away . . .

Stennett turned the whore over, spread her cheeks and slammed his huge penis into her.

From behind, with her blonde hair, he could pretend that she was Lola, Sawyer's woman.

Neither Lola or Sawyer knew that Stennett wanted her, and that he used blonde whores because he could pretend they were her.

One of these days, though, Sawyer would ask him to do something, and the price would be . . . Lola.

Ellie Lennox lay in bed, still angry. Not only had they saddled her with Al Wyatt, but Whitman had the nerve to tell her that the Pinkerton's were going to introduce Wyatt—*Al Wyatt, for Christ's sake*—as the operative in charge. As if the railroad wouldn't trust a woman to be in charge.

Well, she was in charge, and she was going to make sure Wyatt knew it.

After a moment, as she calmed down, she started to see the advantage to having Wyatt thought to be the op in charge. She would be operating under cover, seen as just another passenger.

After all was said and done, that was the kind of job Ellie longed for, something undercover, where she could show her true talents.

This whole fiasco might end up working out for the best, after all!

SIXTEEN

The next morning Clint awoke and went down to have breakfast in the hotel dining room. He'd found that their food was good, but that their coffee was excellent, black and strong, just as he liked it.

He was having his first cup, waiting for his breakfast to arrive, when he saw a man enter the dining room, look around, and then apparently focus on him.

The man was small, well-dressed, in his early fifties by all appearances. Ostensibly, he presented no threat, but as he began to walk toward Clint, he let his hand drop to his gun.

After all, in Deadwood, Hickok had been shot dead by a man who, by all appearances, presented no threat to anyone.

"Excuse me, Mr. Adams?" the man asked.

"That's right."

"I wonder if I might be able to have a word with you?" The man offered his business card, and Clint took it. It had a huge, open eye in the center and said: RAY WHITMAN, PINKERTON.

"Have a seat, Mr. Whitman."

As the small man sat, Clint couldn't help but wonder

if old Allan had changed his qualifications somewhat.

"What's on old Allan's mind?"

"Old Allan?" the man said. "Oh, I see. You're ac-quainted with Mr. Pinkerton?"

"Yes, I am."

They hadn't told Whitman that. The little man won-dered why. He also wondered why he was being used for this instead of someone else.

"Well, I'm Mr. Pinkerton's—that is, William Pink-erton's—executive assistant."

"So?"

At that moment Clint's breakfast came, and the con-versation lapsed until it was served.

"Can I get you anything?" Clint asked Whitman.

"No, nothing. Thank you."

The waiter left.

"Do you mind?" Clint asked, gesturing at his plate.

"No, of course not. Please, eat your breakfast."

"While I'm eating, tell me what I can do for you?"

Whitman paused. Pinkerton had told him to try and find out why Adams was in Chicago but to be discreet. Whitman had argued that he was not a field man, but Pinkerton had insisted that he had confidence in his assistant.

"Just talk to him, man," William had said. "You don't need field experience for that."

"Mr. Whitman?"

"Yes?"

"*Is* there something I can do for you?"

"Well, I was just wondering—"

"Don't you mean Allan was wondering?"

"I told you, I work for William—"

"William, Allan, it's all the same thing, Mr. Whitman—may I call you, Ray?"

"Uh, er, yes, of course."

"Ray, can I make this easier on you?"

"I don't know what you mean."

"Didn't Allan—that is, William—tell you to try and find out what I was doing in Chicago?"

"I'm sorry, but—"

"He probably also told you to be discreet."

"Mr. Adams—"

"Have you ever had field experience, Ray?"

"Well . . . no, but—"

"Do you play chess?"

"Chess? Why, yes, I do."

"I think you're being used as a pawn, Ray. You should know that Allan and I are not the best of friends. I think he had William send you to talk to me *because* of your inexperience."

"What do you mean?"

"Well, they obviously felt that you would pose no apparent threat to me and that I might let my guard down. What do you think of that?"

"I'm sure I don't know . . ." Whitman began, but he let it trail off, looking a bit put out.

In point of fact, Whitman was put out. This was out of his field of expertise. He was an administrative man, not a field man. He also didn't like being used "as a pawn" as Clint Adams put it.

He stood up.

"I'm sorry for bothering you, Mr. Adams."

"Oh now, don't go away mad, Ray. You're not thinking of doing something silly, like resigning?"

"I—" Whitman said, then firmed his jaw and said, "The thought had crossed my mind."

"You haven't dealt much with Allan Pinkerton, have you?" Clint asked.

"No. I have been working with William Pinkerton."

"How does he treat you?"

"Fine, when . . ." Whitman started, but he let it trail off without finishing the thought.

"When Allan isn't around?" Clint said, prompting him a little.

Whitman hesitated, then nodded.

"Look Ray, keep your job. It's probably a good one, right? You'd have a hard time finding one like it?"

"Yes."

"Then forget about Old Allan. He'll be gone soon, and William will be back in control. For now, just go back and tell William what he wants to know."

"What's that?"

"Tell him I'm here to go on a train ride."

"Were those his exact words?" Allan asked William. William Pinkerton had asked Ray Whitman that only minutes earlier.

"Yes, Father, his exact words."

Allan Pinkerton looked unhappy.

"He's going to be on that train."

"Which one?" William asked.

"The one going from here to Denver, of course."

"So?"

"So I don't like coincidences."

"What do you want to do about it?"

"We still have three days. I want a complete guest list for that train."

"And if Adams isn't on it?"

"Then his being here to go on a train trip would simply be a coincidence."

"But . . . you don't believe in coincidence."

"Exactly right. Can we free up another man to go on the trip? I mean, an operative with experience?"

"I don't think so, Father. Not—"

"Try, William," Allan said. "Try and get me someone who knows what he's doing, eh? Someone who won't give himself away? Otherwise, I might have to go myself."

"Father, not with your health—"

"Then get me somebody!"

William sighed and knew his father meant it.

"All right, Father," he said, "I'll do my best. We have another problem, though."

"And what's that?"

"Ray Whitman. He's a little upset about the way we used him."

"Soothe him."

"Father—"

"So give him a raise."

"Father, somehow I don't think a simple raise is going to—"

"How effective is he at what he does?"

"Very effective," William said after a moment. "He's an excellent administrator—"

"Then give him a big raise, William, and apologize to him. Blast it, I don't have time for problems with subordinates, right now. Just get out of here and get me a good man," he said, waving his hand at his son, "someone who can stay on Adams without being seen."

"I'll do my best, Father."

After William left the office—*his* office—Allan Pinkerton lit up one of his cigars. He leaned back and drew the smoke deeply into his lungs. He doubted very much that they had a man in the Chicago office who was good enough to stay with Adams without being noticed.

This was one of those times—those rare times—that he wished he still had Talbot Roper to call on.

SEVENTEEN

There were four people in the Richard Sawyer's room. He and Lola, naturally. The other two were Pete Bateman and Lenny Germaine.

Bateman had been the first to arrive and had just been given a drink by Lola when there was a knock on the door and Germaine entered. He was also given a drink, and then both men looked expectantly at Sawyer.

"We're waiting for one more person," he told them.

"Who?" Bateman asked.

"That remains to be seen," Sawyer said. "Why don't you fellas have a seat."

So they all sat for a half hour that way until Bateman and Germaine began exchanging impatient glances. Finally, they seemed to silently agree that Bateman would ask.

"Sawyer—" he started, but he was interrupted by a knock on the door.

Now it was Sawyer and Lola who exchanged glances, because only they knew what the knock on the door meant. Lola didn't look happy, but Sawyer's face took on a look of great satisfaction.

He opened the door and Tom Stennett walked in. Bateman and Germaine both knew Stennett, and they both had the same attitude toward him. He was a killer, and the less time they had to spend with him the better.

Stennett's eyes moved around the room until they fell on Lola. She seemed to be the only one who noticed, and she shivered. They paused on her for a moment, and then he looked at Sawyer.

"I'm here."

"I can see that, Stennett," Sawyer said. "Welcome aboard." He looked at the others and said, "Now we can get down to business."

They drilled for three days, and on the third day Sawyer brought in the gunhands, five men who would simply point their guns where they were told to point them.

"Are you sure you can get us aboard?" Pete Bateman asked.

"Lola is coming as my guest," Sawyer explained, "although I'll make sure she gets a cabin of her own. Germaine will be coming as the Count Germaine, from Russia. They won't turn him away if he shows up with me. They wouldn't want to risk an international incident. Bateman, you and Stennett will be the Count's bodyguards. There won't be any need for either of you to speak, by the way."

"That suits me," Stennett said.

"Lenny, did you get the clothes?"

"I've got them."

"Good. What about your accent?"

"I'll drop a few V's into my speech pattern and use

a few gutteral vowels. I don't think we'll have any problem."

"What about getting these five aboard?"

"That's the dicey part," Sawyer said. "Revealing ourselves has to be timed just right, so that we can stop the train and let them board."

"And if we miss?" Bateman asked.

"Then we'll do it ourselves, without them. They'll get paid, anyway."

The five gunhands seemed to like that part.

"You fellas have your part down?"

They all nodded.

"Okay, then you can leave. Will some luck, we'll be seeing you in two days."

They waited as the five men filed out.

"All right," Sawyer said, "there's one more thing I have to tell you."

"What?" Bateman asked.

"I've had somebody watching the office of the head of this railroad."

"Why?"

"I want to see who goes in and out."

"You're interested in who they're going to get for security," Stennett said.

Sawyer smiled.

"That's right."

"They'll go to Pinkerton, won't they?" Lenny Germaine asked. "I mean, wouldn't you?"

"I would," Sawyer said, "because they have the best reputation, and they certainly are going to Pinkerton. That's no surprise."

Bateman narrowed his eyes.

"Then what is the surprise, Sawyer?"

"I've gotten word that there was an interesting visitor to the railroad office."

"Who?" Bateman asked. "Or do you intend to keep us in suspense?"

"Clint Adams."

Everybody in the room recognized the name, but it was Stennett who seemed to react more. He straightened up suddenly but did not say anything.

"The Gunsmith?" Bateman said.

"That's right."

"He's gonna be on this train?" Lenny the German asked.

"It's possible," Sawyer said, "and if he is, I don't want it to be a surprise to anyone."

"But . . . what do we do about him?" Bateman asked.

"We don't do anything," Sawyer said, looking at Stennett. "That's Stennett's job."

Stennett simply looked at Sawyer and ignored the others.

"Bateman? Lenny?" Sawyer said. "Any questions?"

Bateman wanted to ask if Stennett could handle the Gunsmith, but he decided against it. He had too much healthy respect—and fear—for Stennett to ask the question in front of him.

"Yeah," Bateman said. "If we aren't able to get those five on the train, how are we going to be able to control the people?"

"We'll do it."

"How? There will be four of us—"

"Five," Lola said.

"All right," Bateman said, "five of us, and who knows how many people. Somebody's going to try and be a hero for sure."

"Again, that's where Stennett comes in."

"How?"

"He's going to convince people that there's no percentage in trying to be a hero."

"How's he going to do that?"

"By doing what he does best."

Everyone in the room knew what that was.

Killing!

"Any more questions?" Stennett asked.

Bateman and Germaine just shook their heads.

"All right," Sawyer said. "We'll meet back here tomorrow morning. Lenny, in costume, all right?"

"Sure."

"Bateman, just wear dark clothes."

"Right."

Bateman and Germaine moved to the door to leave, but Stennett didn't move from his seat.

EIGHTEEN

Sawyer and Lola exchanged glances, and then Sawyer said, "Stennett? Have you got something on your mind?"

"Another drink, for one thing."

Sawyer looked at Lola, who walked over to Stennett to pour him another drink. Their eyes met as she poured, and even though there was no expression on Stennett's face, she shivered again. It was as if his eyes projected a coldness that chilled her to the bone, and yet there was also a heat. For the first time since she had met Stennett—and she had seen him on and off for the past three years—she felt something other than revulsion for him.

Could it have been . . . desire?

The very thought that she could *want* him that way revolted her, and yet when she turned away from him she was acutely aware of the heat between her legs.

God, she was wet . . .

"Tell me something," Stennett said to Sawyer.

Lola replaced the whiskey bottle on the small portable bar and then made a concerted effort not to look at Stennett.

"What?" Sawyer asked.

"You've got a lot of money, right? I mean, you're bankrolling this job, just like you've bankrolled every other we've worked on."

"What's your point?" Sawyer asked.

"What do you get out of this?" Stennett asked. "I mean, you can't be doing it for the money."

"Have you ever had a lot of money, Stennett?" Sawyer asked. "I mean, a *lot* of money."

"Not the kind of money you're talking about."

"Well, take my word for it," Sawyer aid. "It's boring. I need excitement, and my chosen profession provides it."

Stennett stared at Sawyer for a few moments, then finished his drink and set the glass aside. He stood up and walked to the door.

"My end is bigger than theirs, right?" he asked, meaning Bateman and Germaine.

"You'll get your usual cut."

"And bonus?"

"And bonus," Sawyer said, nodding.

"I'll need a litle bigger bonus than usual this time, Sawyer."

"Why?"

"The Gunsmith."

"I should think it would be bonus enough that you're getting a shot at him, Stennett."

"That's easy for you to say," Stennett said. "You won't have to face him."

"Can you handle him?" Sawyer asked.

"You just be ready to give me an extra bonus."

"Like what?"

For a fleeting moment Lola caught Stennett looking at her, and she shivered.

"I'll let you know," Stennett said, and left.

"Rich," Lola said.

"What?"

"Take me to bed."

"Lola, we—"

There was a desperate edge to her voice when she repeated, "Take me to bed."

"I still have some things to go over, Lola. Go inside and I'll join you shortly."

She knew she wouldn't be able to change his mind, so she went into the bedroom, stripped, and laid down on the bed. Slowly, she slid her hand down her body until her fingers were resting between her legs, where it was hot and wet . . .

Against her will—against her better judgment—she began to move her fingers and . . . God help her . . . she thought about Stennett . . .

"This is crazy," Pete Bateman said to Lenny Germaine when they reached the street.

"What is?"

"Robbing a train that has the Gunsmith on it."

"What if he isn't gonna be on it?"

Bateman laughed shortly.

"Then Sawyer wouldn't have brought it up."

"You don't think Stennett can take him?"

"I don't know, but I wouldn't bet my life on it," Bateman said.

"You want to pull out?"

"No, but I might want to change the odds a little."

"How?"

Bateman looked at Lenny Germaine and said, "By making sure the Gunsmith isn't on that train."

NINETEEN

When Althea Saunders answered the knock on her door she staggered back as Sam Grain pushed his way in.

"Sam, what—" she started, but he slapped her across the face with the flat of his hand, so as not to leave a mark. Her head rocked back, and she staggered back even farther and fell to the floor at the foot of her bed.

"Sam, what are you doing?"

"Disciplining you, girl," he said.

"I don't understand," she said.

"You haven't seen Clint Adams in three days."

"I—I couldn't. My mother—"

"Sure, your mother was sick. Bitch!" he said, reaching down and taking her by the hair. "When I tell you to do something, I expect you to do it. You're gonna learn that."

The blows came hard and fast. Althea tried to cough out a protest, but all she could do was grunt in pain.

When Grain released her, she fell to the floor.

"Now, Allie," he said, breathing hard. "I want you to go and see Clint Adams."

"I'll be seeing him tomorrow, on the train," she

said. She wanted Grain to leave so she could crawl into bed.

"You'll go and see him tonight. Tell him what you tried to tell me, that your mother was sick. Make him believe that you missed him. I want you and him to be real close on this trip."

She nodded, muttering, "All right."

"And don't forget your real job, keeping tabs on Forrest for me."

"Yes."

Grain turned and went to the door.

"Tell me something?" he asked.

"What?" she replied, without looking up at him.

"Hasn't he ever tried to take you to bed? Forrest, I mean?"

"No."

"Not once?"

"Not once," she said. "He loves his wife."

"Interesting," Grain said. "It would be interesting to use you to test him and see just how much he really does love his wife."

She looked at him then, with loathing. She liked Forrest Evers, hated spying on him, and would hate even more to try and take him from his wife.

"Be real interesting," Grain said, and left.

Sitting there on the floor, Althea vomited onto the floor.

TWENTY

The night before the trip, Sawyer and Lola went to bed together, but even as Sawyer's rigid penis was sliding up between Lola's legs the vision of Tom Stennett came to her, unbidden . . . unwanted . . . unavoidable.

The orgasm she had that night eclipsed any she'd ever had before.

It frightened her.

Sawyer rolled off Lola, glad that she had enjoyed herself. It would be a while before he'd be able to give her more of the same. Of course, she'd probably find herself some young stud on the train, but he knew that would only be to scratch an itch. It wouldn't mean anything more to her than a quick roll in the hay.

Stennett made use of the same blonde whore again, but his thoughts were of Lola—or whatever her real name was. He was sure that something had passed between them in Sawyer's room.

He'd never wanted a woman as badly as he wanted her.

There just might be an *extra* bonus for him at the end of this job.

• • •

"What's wrong, dear?" Helen Evers asked.

Forrest Evers was standing at the window of their bedroom, looking out at the street below.

"Can't sleep," he said shortly.

"You're just excited about tomorrow. Don't worry, everything will go well."

"I'm sure it will, Helen. Go back to sleep."

"You'd better get some rest, darling."

"I will. Go back to sleep."

As his wife turned over to make herself comfortable, Forrest Evers took a deep breath, trying to quell the pain in his stomach. All he needed was for Grain, the railroad, and this trip to give him an ulcer.

Excited, Helen had said. Excitement wasn't quite what he was feeling.

Fear, now that was more like it.

In a hotel room across town, a slender, pale, almost frail young man in his mid-twenties sat a writing desk and worked furiously with pen and ink, getting his thoughts down on paper. Recently he had published a record of his journeys through southern France, called *Travels with a Donkey*. Tomorrow, he would be traveling by rail from Chicago to Denver, and he would be writing about that, as well, for his journals about his travels across North America by steam car.

His name was Robert Louis Stevenson.

Althea Saunders cuddled closer to Clint Adams as he slept. Sex with Clint had all but wiped away the memory of what Sam Grain had done to her. Clint Adams thought as much of her pleasure as he did of his own. She had never met a man like that before.

She hoped he wouldn't end up hating her *too* much.

• • •

Clint awoke abruptly, and attributed it to that survival instinct that had kept him alive for so long. He had heard something without realizing that he had heard it, and now he lay still and listened intently.

And heard it again.

A scratchy sound, like metal against metal.

Someone was trying to unlock the door to the room without the use of a key.

He slid his legs off the bed without waking Althea and drew his gun from the holster on the bedpost. As he did so he heard the lock click and hurriedly pushed Althea from the bed to the floor.

The door slammed open, and a man's silhouette showed in the doorway. He fired his gun at the bed four times and then Clint fired once, striking the man squarely in the chest. The assailant staggered backward, into the hallway, and fell to the floor.

"What in the world—" Althea was sputtering as Clint got up and moved to the doorway. He looked out only long enough to make sure the man was dead and then closed the door.

"What happened?" Althea asked, getting to her feet.

"You'd better get dressed," Clint said.

"Why?"

"Unless I miss my guess," he said, "we'll be having a visit from the police."

"Will we be going to jail?"

"I'm sure we won't," Clint said, putting his gun back into his holster. "We'll just have some explaining to do."

"I hope it doesn't keep us from missing the train in the morning."

"It won't," he assured her, "but that might have been the general idea."

TWENTY-ONE

Forrest Evers was at the railroad depot very early, so as to be able to greet all of his guests personally.

Among the first to arrive were Angela Warren, the famed stage actress; William Dunne, the famed actor, who hated Angela as much as she hated him; Walter Kemp, the industrialist; Mr. and Mrs. Raleigh Kind, the son and daughter-in-law of one of Chicago's richest men; Robert Louis Stevenson, a young writer; Sam "Bull" Gifford, probably the next heavyweight champion of the boxing world; Dr. George Murrow, a prominant chicago physician; and Senator Joseph Creighton, and his "companion," a busty young woman named Florence "Flower" Muldoon.

Evers was watching the arrivals nervously, awaiting his guests, but also awaiting the arrival of William Pinkerton and the "agent in charge."

Finally, they arrived.

Evers recognized Pinkerton immediately. Walking alongside him was a tall, rather powerfully built man who looked as if his shoulders were going to burst from his suit. At least, Evers thought, he looked formidable.

"I'm so glad you've arrived," Evers said as the two men reached him.

"Mr. Evers, this is Al Wyatt. He will be the agent in charge."

"Mr. Wyatt," Evers said, extending his hand, which became lost in the other man's.

"Mr. Evers," the man said in a deep base, "you've got nothing to worry about."

"I really wish you'd let me know how many agents you have aboard," Evers said.

"That won't be necessary, Mr. Evers," Pinkerton said. "In fact, it's probably better that you don't know how many men we have on board. Just relax and let us take care of security for you."

"Yes, yes, of course," Evers said. "Shall I arrange for a cabin—"

"No, Al will ride as just another paying customer," Pinkerton said.

Evers was pleased. He had no cabins to spare.

Pinkerton and Wyatt shook hands, and Pinkerton said, "Good luck."

Pinkerton left, and Al Wyatt gave Evers a reassuring look and stepped on board.

Ellie Lennox was already on board, watching Pinkerton, Wyatt, and Evers from a window. As usual, Wyatt looked very formidable. Nobody could ever tell by looking at the man that he was an idiot.

And nobody would ever be able to tell, just looking at her, that she was a Pinkerton.

Finally, Clint Adams arrived with Althea Saunders, just ahead of Sam Grain.

"Good morning, Clint," Evers greeted him. "Althea, glad you're here."

"Morning, Forrest," Clint said. He and Althea had agreed not to tell Evers anything about the attempt on Clint's life last night. They had straightened it out with the police, and that was all that mattered.

Clink looked around at the normal passenger traffic, the ones who paid their own way because they weren't prominent enough to have been invited.

"Looks like quite a turnout."

"It is, it is."

"Have most of the guests arrived?" Althea asked.

"A good many of them, yes," Evers said, looking around nervously for the rest. Clint noticed that Evers was constantly rubbing his stomach.

"I'm sorry I'm late," she said. Turning to Clint she touched his arm and said, "I'd better get inside and see to them."

He nodded, and she boarded the train.

"How many of these special cars do you have, Forrest?"

"Five," Evers answered, vigorously rubbing his stomach. "Two parlor cars, a dining car, and two sleepers. Uh, you'll have a cabin on one of the sleepers of course."

"Thank you. Uh, Forrest, are you having some stomach trouble?"

"Huh?" Evers looked down at himself, then dropped his hand away from his stomach. "I think I'm getting a damned ulcer. Just what I need, eh?"

"See a doctor."

"Oh, I will, I will, as soon as this trip is over." He looked past Clint and said, "Ah, here's another of the guests—with company, I see. Damn it!" His hand went to his stomach again. "These society people think they can bring—Good morning, Mr. Sawyer."

"Good morning, Evers," Richard Sawyer said. Clint gave the man called Sawyer a glance, and then directed his attention to the blonde on his arm. She was on the far side of thirty, a little hard-edged, but she certainly wore it well. In her youth she must have been a real beauty, for even now she was a dazzler.

"This is my guest, Miss Lorraine Durant."

"Miss Durant."

"To keep you from getting any ideas," Sawyer said, leaning close to Evers, "Miss Durant will have her own cabin."

"Of course," Evers said, and then he looked pointedly at the other men with Sawyer.

"Ah, this is my good friend Count Germaine, here on a visit from Russia. I knew you wouldn't object to having him along."

"No, of course not," Evers said.

Count Germaine snapped his heels together and bowed shortly.

"It is my pleasure to ride your vonderful train, Mr. Evers. I am most looking vorward to it."

"It's our pleasure to have you abroad Count—uh, you and your, uh—"

"My . . . bodyguards. Vould that they could be called something else, but . . ." the Count said, spreading his hands and giving a fatalistic shrug.

"Of course, of course. Please, step aboard."

As Sawyer and his friends boarded, Evers said, "I'm sorry I didn't introduce you. You'll meet everyone when we get on board. Oh, Jesus!"

"What?"

"I don't have a cabin for that Count. I've got to get on board and tell Althea to charm him while I—"

"Don't worry, Forrest," Clint said. "You can give him my cabin."

"Truly? You don't mind?"

"Nah. I'll try one of those reclining seats you told me about."

"Well, sure, anything you want, Clint. Thanks. I've got to tell Althea."

"Go ahead."

"If any of the other guests arrive—there are only a few—"

"I'll try to fill in until you get back."

"Great—oh, shit!" Now he clutched at his stomach, as if he'd been stabbed.

"Now what?"

Evers was looking past Clint at someone, and the look on his face was not a happy one.

"Grain."

"Who?"

"Sam Grain, my partner. He's not supposed to be here. He said he wasn't coming." His tone of voice sounded like a man betrayed, and his hand was clutching at his stomach.

If Evers did indeed have an ulcer, Clint wondered how much his partner had contributed to it.

"Go on, Forrest," he said, putting his hand on the man's shoulder. "I'll introduce myself."

"Thanks," Evers said for what seemed like the umpteenth time.

Clint turned and waited for the big, well-dressed man in his fifties to reach him. Grain looked like a man who had been in fine shape in his youth, but of late everything he ate seemed to have gone to his belly.

"Mr. Grain?"

The man stopped short and looked at Clint with the expression of someone who was trying to figure out whether or not he knew someone.

"That's right."

"My name's Clint Adams."

"Oh, yes. You're Forrest's Western friend. What do they call you? The Gunsmith, isn't that it?"

"Uh, yeah, right."

"Yeah, you're a regular legend of the west, aren't you? Like Wild Bill Hickok!"

"Not quite."

Grain stuck his hand out, and Clint reluctantly took it. He didn't like the man. As he suspected, Grain tried to exert pressure in an impromptu test of strength. When Clint matched him, the man released his hand and put both of his behind his back.

"It looks like you've got a real nice turnout, Mr. Grain. Real nice. You should be pleased."

"Oh, I am, Mr. Adams," Grain said. "I'm so pleased that I've decided to go along."

"Really? I understood that there were no more cabins in the sleeper cars."

"Is that a fact?"

"As a matter of fact, I've just given up mine in favor of some Russian count."

"Interesting," Grain said. "Well, the cabins have two berths. I'm sure Forrest won't mind sharing his with me. After all, we are partners. See you aboard, Adams."

"Sure."

With the agitated state that Forrest Evers was obviously in, the last thing he needed was to share his cabin with a partner he didn't like.

That was the problem with partners, Clint thought.

All the ones he ever knew ended up disliking each other.

The only partner he'd ever had was Duke, the big black gelding who was now in the care of Rick Hartman, back in Labyrinth, Texas. Rick had often offered Clint a partnership in his holdings—especially his saloon in Labyrinth. Clint had just seen another reason for him to keep refusing. As long as they weren't partners, he and Rick would remain friends.

A carriage pulled up at the depot, and two people stepped down from it. One was a man in his early sixties, and the other, a woman in her forties whose full figure was just starting to go on her. Still, she was a handsome sight, and he wondered if she was the man's wife.

He stepped forward to find out. He was, after all, unofficial greeter.

Actually, unofficially, he was much more than that, but he wouldn't find out about that until much later on.

TWENTY-TWO

When Clint finally boarded the train, it looked like a three-ring circus. The normal passenger cars were crowded, with people moving through the aisles looking for seats. Some of them, he heard, were there simply to catch a glimpse of some famous person, like the actress or the prize fighter.

When he reached the first parlor car, it was a little less crowded and much more organized. He could also see how expensive everything was. The wood was hand carved, the furniture well padded, and there was lots of gold and silver plating. There were two waiters circulating with trays of drinks and snacks. Clint looked around and didn't see either Evers or Grain, but he did see Althea, and went to join her.

"Sam Grain is aboard," he told her.

"Really? Is he coming along?"

"Yes. Forrest is upset."

"I'm sure he is. He and Sam aren't exactly the best of friends, even though they're partners."

Clint wondered if Althea called all of her boss's partners by their first name.

"Let me introduce you to some people," Althea said.

"Later. I'm going to have to stake out one of those reclining seats in here."

"Most of these people have cabins. There'll be some paying passengers in here later, but you don't have to worry about that."

"Why?"

"Silly," she told him. "You can sleep in my cabin."

"Now that," he said, "is an interesting proposition."

"I thought you might see it that way."

"What's happening in the next car?"

"The same thing. Once we get underway meals will be served in the special dining car, but there will be drinks and snacks served in both these parlor cars."

"And the paying customers in here?"

"The ones that can afford it. The people in the regular passenger cars will eat in the regular dining car."

"This is all getting too confusing for me."

She laughed and put her hand on his arm.

"Let me introduce you to some people," she said again, and this time he agreed.

She introduced him to some businessmen, some of Chicago's upper crust, someone she referred to as an industrialist, and young man who was a writer. The only name he managed to retain was the writer's, because it was so distinctive. Robert Louis Stevenson. He was a young man, small and frail, and obviously very intelligent. Clint hoped to be able to talk to him at length later.

"Let's go into the next car," she said. "Forrest and Sam will be entertaining in there. I'll free them up to come in here."

"When do we get underway?"

"Shortly."

"How long is this trip going to take?"

"As I understand it, Forrest has arranged for us to arrive in Denver tomorrow night. We won't be travel-ing at top speed. Some of these people will be getting their first look at the plains. They want to see some buffalo, and cowboys and Indians."

"Good luck to them."

"Why?"

"There are hardly any more buffalo to see. As far as Indians, we'd be better off not seeing any."

Althea led the way to the next parlor car where they found Forrest talking to the man and woman who had arrived almost last.

"That's Mr. and Mrs. Winston Judd," Althea said.

"I know. I met them on their way in."

"He's in high finance, owns a bank or two, and she—well, she's a barracuda."

"I beg your pardon?"

"What happened when you met?"

"Uh, I believe the lady was giving me the once over."

"She'll feed on you, if you're not careful, like a barracuda."

"Why did he marry a younger woman?"

"Older men like to have beautiful young wives."

"She must have been very beautiful, at one time."

"Don't kid me. Even at forty-one—which she claims to be—she's an attractive woman."

"Claims to be?"

"How many women do you know who can get mar-ried at twenty, and twenty-seven years later be forty-one?"

He smiled and said, "All the women I've ever met could accomplish that very nicely."

She punched him on the arm and said, "Come on, let's rescue Forrest. He's got other guests to tend to."

When Althea and Clint interrupted Forrest Evers and the Judds, Clint abruptly felt as if he were being undressed by Heather Judd's eyes. He felt that "Heather" might have been a good name for a young girl, but for a matronly woman in her mid-forties, it was absurd.

He refrained from saying so, however.

"You have other guests to look after, Mr. Evers," Althea said. "I can help Mr. and Mrs. Judd."

"Very well, Althea. I will see both of you later."

As Evers left Mrs. Judd gave Althea an up and down look and said, "I doubt that there is anything you could help me with, my dear."

"Now, dear," her husband began, but the woman took her husband's arm and pulled him away with her, giving Clint a sloe-eyed glance over her shoulder.

"That woman has her eye on you, Clint," Althea said. "Definitely."

"I may not have to sleep in your cabin," he said, "as much as hide out in it."

TWENTY-THREE

Eventually Clint became separated from Althea and had to fend for himself. In his own opinion, he did quite nicely. He had some concern about whether or not he'd be able to sustain a conversation with people with whom he had nothing in common. To his surprise, several of the people knew who he was and peppered him with questions, so it did not fall to him to try and sustain or stimulate conversation.

Finally, as he might have expected, he was cornered by Heather Judd—without her husband.

"So, you've managed to get away from that clutching female."

"What female is that, Mrs. Judd?"

She moved in close to him, and he couldn't avoid chest to chest contact without literally pushing her away—and she had a very nice, cushiony chest to make contact with. It also gave him a close look at the diamond necklace she was wearing. It had to be worth a fortune.

"Oh, Clint—may I call you Clint?"

"Please do."

"If we're going to make this trip together, you're going to have to call me Heather."

"Heather," he said.

She wrinkled her very handsome nose and said, "It's a terrible name, I know."

"It's not so bad."

"You're sweet," she said, touching his face, "but for a woman my age, it is an embarrassment, but what can I do? It's my name."

"Then there's nothing to be embarassed about, and you shouldn't let anybody make you feel that there is."

For a moment Heather Judd's face lost its lascivious, somewhat vapid expression and became almost thoughtful.

"I never thought of it that way," she said, her eyes looking at something only she could see.

"Try it for a while."

She looked at him again, expressionless, and suddenly the "barracuda" was back.

"I think you and I are going to get along very well."

She pressed against him even tighter and began to move her hands, when suddenly Clint saw her husband behind her.

"There you are, my dear," he said, smiling. It was as if he didn't see what anyone else would have seen, his wife pressing her ample body up against another man.

To Clint, Heather Judd's face looked as if someone had just cast a shadow over it. She backed away from him—just barely—and then turned to face her husband. She was almost as tall as Clint and, as she turned, her hair tickled his nose. It smelled very pleasant. In fact, she might have been a pleasant diversion if it had not been for her husband and Althea Saunders being aboard.

Clint took advantage of the situation to slip by

Heather Judd—although he was unable to do so without brushing against her firm backside. He wondered if she would interpret that as a "see you later" touch.

He moved about the car, picking a glass of champagne off a waiter's tray. He tasted it, then decided he'd much rather have had a beer.

He was looking for someplace to put the champagne down when he saw the young writer, Stevenson.

"Mr. Stevenson."

The man looked up at the sound of his name. His eyes were very mild behind the lenses of his wire-frame glasses. When he saw Clint he frowned for a moment, then recognized him.

"Mr. Adams, isn't it?"

"That's right."

"I understand you enjoy some notoriety, Mr. Adams, I apologize for not recognizing your name, but I have spent a great deal of time abroad."

"That's all right, Mr. Stevenson," Clint said. "The kind of notoriety I 'enjoy,' I do not really enjoy."

"I believe I understand. What kind of reputation is it that you have?"

Clint frowned.

"Is this painful for you to discuss?" Stevenson asked.

"Somewhat. Uh, you're not the kind of writer that Ned Buntline is, are you?"

"Ned Buntline?"

"He writes, uh, dime novels. You know, stories building up legends of the West?"

"Ah, I believe I have seen such things, but they are hardly novels, are they? Aren't they rather slim, published on cheap paper—"

"That's them."

"I can't say I've read any. Do you mean that you've had those kind of novels written about you?"

"I have."

"And this doesn't please you?"

"It does not. I have enough people wanting to try me out without having those kind of books instigating even more confrontations."

"What kind of confrontations? What do you mean by 'trying' you out?"

"With a gun."

"Ah, I did notice your gun. It is rather odd to wear a gun on your hip in Chicago, isn't it?"

"It's very odd, I suppose," Clint said, "but I'm not staying in Chicago long enough to get into trouble for it."

"You are wearing it on this trip, though."

"The kind of reputation I have, I would be foolish not to wear my gun, Mr. Stevenson."

"Please, call me Robert."

"And my name is Clint."

"Clint, we should talk more. Perhaps some writer should put your story down on paper the way it really occurred, and not in a sensationalized form."

"I don't mean to offend you, Robert, but I've never met a writer I thought I could trust enough to talk freely to."

"Ah, that is unfortunate. Well, perhaps we should talk, in any case. I find you a very interesting man. Not what I expected from a . . . a frontiersman."

"I'm hardly a frontiersman."

"A westerner, then. I'm sorry, but being from the East and spending a lot of time abroad, I know very little of the West. That is why I am taking this trip in the first place. Perhaps you would be kind enough to act as a sort of an unofficial guide?"

"I don't know about being a guide, but I'd be perfectly willing to answer any questions you might have."

"Splendid, splendid. I shall look forward to it."

"So will I." Clint looked beyond Stevenson and saw Heather Judd, sans husband, apparently looking for someone—and he thought he knew who.

"Excuse me, I want to check out the other car."

"Certainly . . ." Stevenson, turning his head in puzzlement to see what was coming up behind him.

Clint moved quickly between cars to the next parlor car, where he found much the same thing going on. It looked for all the world like a party, but the kind of cocktail party he had seen taking place in San Francisco or New York.

A waiter came by offering him champagne, but he refused this time. In rapid succession he found himself talking to an actor, a politician, and finally, the prizefighter.

"I guess maybe I've taken as many people out with my fists as you have with your guns, Gunsmith," the boxer eventually said, something Clint had been afraid was coming.

He reacted badly, anyway.

"My name is Adams, Clint Adams," he said, enunciating very carefully, as if speaking to a child.

"Hey, I ain't no dummy . . ." the boxer began, but Clint turned and walked away from him. "Hey, who's he think he's walking away from . . ." he heard the man say to someone.

Maybe he reacted wrongly whenever someone called him "Gunsmith." After all, it wasn't really their fault. It was, after all, what they knew about him, and what they assumed he was called, but he couldn't help but cringe whenever he heard or even read the name.

Maybe Stevenson was right. Maybe someone should tell his story the way it really was, the story of a young man who had fostered a reputation, without realizing it, through his interest in guns, and the older man who had to live with it.

Maybe Robert Louis Stevenson was the man to write it.

TWENTY-FOUR

Ellie Lennox felt out of place. She had worn her best traveling suit, and still she felt grossly outclassed by the clothing of the people around her. She hoped that she didn't stand out too badly.

She milled about in one of the cars, drinking champagne and listening to people talk. When she saw Clint Adams enter the car, her heart started to beat faster. She felt a smile starting to break out on her face, and she wanted to rush across the car to him when she remembered who she was and why she was there.

She was going to have to talk to Clint, all right, but in private and before he could give her away. She started to move slowly across the car when she saw Clint moving toward—of all people—that idiot, Al Wyatt.

Clint found himself face to face with a man who could have been a boxer. He wondered if there were two of them on the train.

"Hello," the man said. His voice was a deep rumbling bass, and he had a pair of shoulders even Bull Gifford would envy.

"My name's Clint Adams," Clint said, extending his hand.

"Mine's Wyatt, Al Wyatt." The big man shook hands without starting a test of strength.

"What did you do to get invited on this jaunt?" Clint asked.

"Uh, well, I, uh—" Wyatt stammered. He had quickly forgotten what Pinkerton had told him would be his cover. He started looking around the room for Ellie Lennox, and if he had seen her would certainly have given her away.

"Mr. Wyatt?"

"I just, uh, came along for the ride," Wyatt said, sweat beading up on his forehead. "Excuse me, I'd like to get something to drink."

He pushed past Clint, who stared after him wondering if he was ill.

Ellie had time to step behind a group of people who were talking about seeing "real red savages," which kept her from being seen by either Al Wyatt or Clint Adams.

As Wyatt staggered by, looking nervous, Ellie decided that he must have made a fool of himself. She was going to have to get to Clint to undo any damage Wyatt might have done.

Clint was still wondering what Al Wyatt's problem was when he saw Ellie Lennox approaching him. She was dressed in a rather severe gray traveling suit, and her hair was pulled back into a bun. Since it was obviously not the way she would normally dress, he was in no danger of giving her away. He knew she had to be working.

"Please," she said as she came close to him, "don't say anything—"

"Do I know you?" he asked.

She frowned, almost said his name, and then realized what he was doing.

"I don't think so," she said. "My name is Ellen Lennox."

"Clint Adams."

"Mr. Adams . . . I need a little air. Would you mind accompanying me outside, between the cars, perhaps?"

"Of course," he said. "I wouldn't want you to fall off."

"We're not moving, yet," she said.

He smiled and said, "I know."

Once they were outside the instinct for both of them was to kiss, but they were plainly visible from the platform and that would not have been wise. Clint did, however, risk a reassuring grip on her forearm.

"Thanks for not giving me away," she said.

"Unless this is the way you dress and wear your hair now, there was no danger of that."

"I should have known you'd think first before saying anything. What did Wyatt say to you?"

"Nothing. He seemed sort of . . . at a loss—"

"He's an idiot!"

"Is he—he isn't—"

"Yes, he is," she said. "I can't believe they've saddled me with him, but they have. Not only that, but they've introduced him to Forrest Evers as the agent in charge."

"And you are really the agent in charge?"

"Yes."

"For security."

"Yes."

"How many agents do you have on board, Ellie?"

"This is not generally known," she said. "I mean, Evers hasn't been informed—"

"Just the two of you?" Clint guessed.

She stared at him a moment, then nodded helplessly.

"I guess Allan isn't taking this jaunt very seriously, is he?"

"I think he's only supplying security for political reasons," she said, "but I'm determined to supply as much as I can with what I have."

"Which isn't much."

"No," she said, "unless—"

"Unless what?"

"Unless you're willing to help."

"Oh, I'm willing," he said, smiling. "In fact, I think this has sort of been inevitable."

"What do you mean?"

He explained how he met Evers and was invited to take part in the trip.

"I think now I know why."

"Why?"

He explained further that a lot of people on board knew who he was.

"Wait a minute. You think Evers has invited you along, and then let people know who you were to try and keep anyone from trying anything?"

"That's what I think."

"Aren't you angry?"

"How can I be angry?" he asked. "If he hadn't invited me I wouldn't be seeing you right now."

She smiled somewhat shyly and said, "You always know the right things to say." In her present position, however, she couldn't afford to be reduced by Clint's presence to a shy or lovesick young woman. "I don't think we'll be able to see much of one another during this trip."

"There's always Denver," he said.

"Yes, of course," she said, "Denver." Denver held some nice memories for both of them. "So, I can count on you for help?"

"If you need it, sure."

"Thanks, Clint," she said, touching his arm. "I'm glad you're here."

"So am I."

"I'd better get back inside and remind Wyatt what his cover is."

"What is it?"

"He's supposed to be a member of the press. That would give him the run of the train."

"Makes sense."

"If only he can remember it."

"Good luck."

She smiled, then disappeared inside the car. From the other car Clint could hear Forrest Evers advising visitors to leave the train.

They were about to get underway.

TWENTY-FIVE

Things settled down a bit when the visitors left the train. Preparations for departure were made. Those passengers with sleeper cabins went to them, and the others went to their seats, leaving one of the parlor cars empty, except for Evers, Althea, Clint, and Sam Grain.

"Jesus," Evers said, mopping his brow.

"Relax, Forrest," Sam Grain said. "Everything went fine."

Clint wondered how Grain would know. He'd spent very little time mingling with the guests himself.

Evers looked at Althea who—against her better judgment, Clint knew—was forced to agree with Sam Grain.

"It went well, Mr. Evers."

"I think it went fine," Clint said. "That is, if anyone is interested in my opinion."

Grain looked at Clint and said, "I'm still not clear as to what you're doing here, Mr. Adams. I'd probably give your opinion more value if I knew that."

"He's my guest, Sam," Evers said. "Lay off him."

"I'm not pressuring him—"

"Good," Evers said. "Clint, I'd be pleased if you'd

join me for dinner in my cabin."

"Fine with me," Clint said. "There are a few things I'd like to talk over with you, too."

"Does that dinner include me?" Grain asked.

"No," Forrest said.

"It is my cabin, too."

"It's my cabin, Sam," Evers said. "I'm simply letting you sleep there because you insisted on coming along on the trip. That doesn't mean you have free run of it. Have dinner in the dining car with the other guests."

Grain didn't look happy, but he kept quiet and made a show of lighting a cigar. When he was done, he said, "Maybe I'll have dinner with Althea here. That would certainly be more attractive a proposition than dinner with you two."

"I have a dinner engagement," Althea said.

"Oh? With who?"

"With me," Clint said.

"But you're eating with Forrest."

"And so is Althea."

Grain looked at the three of them, growing red in the face, then gave a forced laugh and stood up.

"I'm going to check out the quality of the liquor on this train."

He left the car.

"I detest that man!" Althea said.

"So do I," Evers said.

"Well, he's not exactly one of my favorite people. I guess that makes it unanimous."

"But he's my partner," Evers said.

"You have other partners, don't you?"

Evers nodded.

"Two, but they're more like silent partners."

"Why don't the three of you buy Grain out?"

Evers laughed, without much humor.

"Grain could buy all three of us and more," Evers said.

"Is he that rich?" Clint asked.

"He is. It was mostly his money that built this railroad, but it was my brains and my sweat," Evers said. "I think that makes it more mine."

"He must have made his investment back by now."

"Investors never make back their investment. The more they get back the more they claim they put in. No, I can't buy Sam out," Evers said, "but there are other ways I can get rid of him."

Clint exchanged glances with Althea, who simply shrugged. She obviously didn't know what her boss meant.

"Well, I'll check out the cabin and make sure there's room for three for dinner."

"That's all right, Forrest," Althea said. "I'm sure Clint just said that to help me out of a tight spot with Sam. I'll have dinner in my cabin."

"Are you sure?"

"I insist," Althea said. "In fact, I'll go and check my cabin, as well."

"When will dinner be?" Clint asked.

"At six?" Evers asked.

That was still a good five hours away.

"Well," Clint said to Althea, "maybe you'll consent to have lunch with me?"

"That sounds like a fine idea," Evers said. "I'll leave you two to plan it."

He left the car.

"What do you know about Forrest and Sam's relationship?" Clint asked.

"Not much," she said. "Only that it's been getting worse and worse since I've been working there, and I'm sure it was going sour before that."

"Do you know what your boss meant about other ways to get rid of him?"

She shook her head and walked over to the over-stuffed chair Clint was sitting in. It had big arms that curved outward, so she was able to sit comfortably on one of them, her hips pressed firmly against his shoulder.

"Right now, I'm more concerned about where we should have this lunch."

"Well, since I was nice enough to give up my cabin," he said, "I thought we might have it in yours."

She gave him a look of mock surprise and said, "Now there's a thought."

TWENTY-SIX

Richard Sawyer had told his people that they'd stay at the "farewell party" as long as everyone else did, so as not to arouse anyone's suspicion, and then they'd meet in his cabin—discreetly.

Lola was the first to arrive and took a seat on Sawyer's berth. Next "Count Germaine" entered with his "bodyguards."

"Isn't this taking a chance?" Lenny asked, dropping his accent.

"No," Sawyer said. "We're all friends here, aren't we? Where is your cabin, Lenny?"

"In the next car."

Sawyer made a face.

"It's all right," he said, as much to himself as the others, "it would have been better if we were in the same car, but it's all right. Lola's is right next door to mine."

"Convenient," Pete Bateman said.

"Yes, isn't it?" Lola said.

"Never mind," Sawyer said. "I assume you all talked to someone out there."

"Lenny did," Bateman said. "Me and Stennett don't know any English, remember?"

"Lola?"

"I talked with a few people."

"Was I exaggerating?"

"Not from what I could see," Lenny said. "I talked to at least two guys who, if they ain't got a million, they ain't that far off."

"The man I talked to wanted to take me to France," Lola said.

"Really?" Sawyer said.

"He said his wife wouldn't mind. He said she enjoyed threesomes."

"These people are a little weird, as well as rich," Lenny observed.

"How much money do you think these people will have with them?" Stennett asked.

They all looked at him.

"Let's face it," he went on, "most of their money is either invested, or in a vault somewhere. How much cash do you expect to come away with?"

"Cash is not what we're after," Sawyer said, "not entirely."

"Did you see the diamonds some of those women were wearing?" Lola asked, a dreamy look coming over her face.

"I did," Sawyer said. "And the bracelets, and the watches and rings some of the men have."

"Do you have a buyer for all that stuff?" Stennett asked.

"That's one of the things I like about you, Stennett. You're so practical."

"Do you?"

"For you, Stennett," Sawyer said, "if I don't have a buyer for the jewelry we get away with, I'll buy the stuff myself."

Stennett stared at Sawyer for a few moments and then smiled, sending chills up and down Lola's spine.

"I'll hold you to that, Sawyer."

Sawyer tried to match Stennett's stare, but felt compelled to look away. He covered it by announcing that they would meet in the dining room and have dinner with all the other guests, "just like normal people."

"There's nothing normal about people who have money," Stennett said, moving toward the door. "You should know that, Sawyer. Come on, Count. It's time to go back to your cabin."

Lenny rose obediently and followed Stennett out of the cabin, followed by Bateman.

"That man scares me," Lola said. "I don't think we should use him anymore, after this."

"I can handle him," Sawyer said. "You'd better go back to your cabin and get some rest."

She stood up and walked over to him, putting her arms around his shoulders.

"Rich—"

"Please, Lola," he said. "I have some thinking to do."

"Sure," she said, "sure you do."

She left his cabin and went next door to her own. As she entered she immediately became aware that she wasn't alone, even though she was closing her door with her back to the room. When she turned she saw him, sitting on her berth.

Stennett.

"What are you doing here?" she demanded.

He just stared at her.

"I asked you what you're doing here."

This time he got up and walked over to her. She was wearing an off-the-shoulder gown that left her

right shoulder bare. He put his hand on it. She was
sure her flesh would crawl, but she was wrong. Instead, she felt a thrill when he touched her—a thrill
she didn't want.

They stared at one another for a while, and then he
said, "Do you want me to leave?"

Yes, she told herself, make him leave.

Yes.

"No."

TWENTY-SEVEN

Clint and Althea decided to forego lunch once they got into her cabin. They had much more of an appetite for each other.

"We'll have to talk to good old Forrest about making the berths a little bigger in here," Clint said as they got into bed together.

Althea pressed herself tightly against him and said, "I'm not complaining."

"Oh, I'm not complaining—" Clint started, but Althea silenced him with a kiss.

In another cabin in the same car, Stennett very slowly peeled Lola's dress to the waist. She wore no corset and her breasts were large and firm, the nipples already distended by her excitement. Stennett took a moment to stare at the pale orbs before speaking.

"You want me, don't you," Stennett said, palming her firm breasts so he could feel the nipples in the center of his hand, "as much as I want you?"

"Yes," she said in a whisper. "God help me, I don't want to, but I do."

"God can't help you now," Stennett said to her, in a tone of voice that chilled her.

He squeezed her breasts, and she closed her eyes and moaned. She thought briefly about Sawyer—the man she loved, or thought she loved—in the next cabin, but then she felt Stennett's lips on her shoulder, moving on her flesh, and she forgot about Sawyer.

She closed her eyes and followed the progress of Stennett's lips by feel as they worked their way down to the slopes of her breasts. He moved one hand away from her nipple so that he could fasten his lips on it, using the hand to cup her breast and bring it up to his mouth. To her complete and utter surprise she experienced an immediate orgasm. No man's attentions had ever brought her to a climax that quickly, that simply.

Her legs felt weak as he sucked her other nipple, and then he peeled the dress off her completely. She was wearing a pair of silk panties, and instead of sliding them down her legs he tore them off her. The quick, violent move made her jump, and then he backed off to take a moment to look at her.

She was breathing heavily, her full, firm breasts rising and heaving. The triangle of hair between her legs was as golden as the hair on her head, and thick. Her waist could have been slimmer—and probably had been when she was younger—and her thighs were a touch too heavy—and probably always had been—but he still wouldn't have changed a thing about her. She was everything he thought she'd be—so far.

When he moved toward her Lola didn't know what to expect, and she was surprised he went to his knees and spread her legs. He probed her with his tongue, eating her while she was still standing.

Stennett was too anxious for her to wait until they were undressed and on the berth together. He'd take her there, too, but later. Now he wanted to taste her, to smell her. He slid his tongue along her moist womanhood, and she spread herself even more to accommodate him.

She looked down at him and realized what a vulnerable position he had put himself in to get to her. She knew the kind of man he was, knew that he was always careful, always on his guard. For him to open himself up to her like this made the situation all the more unbelievable to her. She reached down and ran her fingers through his thick black hair, and when his tongue found her clitoris she came again, so violently that her legs began to give out.

Stennett felt her falling and scooped her up into his arms. He took her to the berth, laid her on it, and undressed in front of her.

This was what he had been waiting three years for.

Althea raised her hips and brought herself down on Clint. His penis slid into her as if it had been covered with butter. She put her hands flat on his chest and began to rotate her hips slowly.

"I don't want you to move," she told him in a husky whisper. "I want to milk it out of you all by myself."

"You hardly need me at all, do you?"

"Oh, yes," she said, closing her eyes and moving her hips faster and faster, "oh, yes . . . I . . . do!"

To Stennett's eyes Lola's flesh almost glowed. He knew she was certainly no virgin, he even knew her past because he'd looked into it without her or Sawyer's knowledge. He knew the good and bad about her, and he knew that she'd been used hard for most of her life. Still, to him she shone, from her hair to her skin, and Lola would have been shocked to know

how much this cold-blooded killer had always wanted
her.

He even knew her real name.

Lola looked at Stennett's body and found that she
liked it. He was rangy, without an ounce of fat, and
she thought he had one of the most beautiful penises
she'd ever seen. It was large and perfectly formed,
and she lost all of her inhibitions as she lowered her
mouth over it and began to suck.

Clint watched Althea's face as she milked him. Her
nostrils flared and her tongue bit into her swollen
lower lip every time she came down on him. Her eyes
were closed, and as her body met his she would moan
aloud, a sound that, oddly, fueled his own excitement.

The woman was incredible in bed. It was too bad
she was a liar.

Stennett let her suck him for a while, then took
hold of her and freed himself from her mouth.

"Please . . ." she said, and it was almost a whimper.
She was more excited by this moment than any other
in her life.

"You get on top," he told her, and that surprised
her. She would have thought that a man like Stennett
would have always wanted to be on top.

She climbed aboard him and took him inside of
her, swallowing him slowly, inch by lovely inch.

He took hold of her hips then and began to move
her up and down on him. She marveled at the strength
in his arms and then she began to help him, finding
the tempo that he apparently wanted.

"Oh, God," she said as she felt another orgasm
building, "Oh, Lord . . ."

"Shh," he told her, "you want Sawyer to hear you?"

"I don't care," she said, and then louder, "I . . . don't . . . care!" and suddenly she was bouncing on him uncontrollably, her entire body shaking.

Just as her orgasm was subsiding, Stennett allowed himself to come, exploding inside of her, and then she was coming again, also, digging her nails into his chest and trying to keep from screaming.

When both of their orgasms had subsided she began to move off him, and he said, "Wait. Don't move."

"What—" she said, but he simply pulled her down to where he could reach her breasts and started licking them. She closed her eyes and arched her back, revelling in the feel of his tongue on her.

Incredibly, as he bit and sucked her nipples she felt him growing inside of her again until he filled her up again.

"Again?" she said, moving on him.

"Again," he said, and took hold of her hips . . .

TWENTY-EIGHT

Ellie Lennox was finding it hard to sit still. She kept walking from one end of the train to the other. She had free access to the more expensive cars, and that meant that everyone else did, too. She figured that if she'd had more men she would have secured them from the rest of the train. After all, that's where a band of robbers would hit, the people with all the money.

And all she had to secure them with was herself, and that idiot Al Wyatt.

She wondered what Clint was doing right at that moment?

Althea turned over and laid down on her back. Clint propped himself up on an elbow and looked down at her.

"It's funny . . ." she said.

"What is?"

She turned her head and looked at him.

"You, coming into my life now."

"Why is that funny?"

"Just when I was convinced that there were no men

in this world that were worth . . . anything, you come
along."

"Why am I different?"

"I've been asking myself that same question."

"All right, then how am I different?"

"I don't know . . . well, for one thing, you're
different in bed. You seem to want me to be as satisfied
as you are."

"That's rare?"

"That, my friend, is unheard of," she told him.
"There are more women than you know that don't like
sex because it's not satisfying."

"And you are one of them?"

"I don't like it when it's not satisfying," she said,
"and it rarely has been for me . . . until now."

"I'm sorry."

"For what?"

"That you've found it unsatisfying in the past."

"And I probably will again, after you . . . leave."

"I hope not," he said, pulling her to him, "I sincerely
hope not."

Ellie entered the second parlor car and found it
empty. Actually, it was just emptying out. She saw
a large man with graying hair exiting the other end,
and she thought she saw someone ahead of him.
Beyond here was the sleeper cars, and then the baggage
cars.

She decided to go and find Al Wyatt and have *him*
check those cars out. After that she was going to get
herself something to eat.

Maybe she was taking this whole thing too seriously, after all.

•   •   •

Lola watched in silence while Stennett dressed, and they exchanged a brief glance before he left. He didn't say anything, but then he didn't have to.

She knew he'd be back.

She stretched her lithe body and then put her hands behind her head. Her breasts ached and her vagina did, too, but she didn't care. It felt marvelous. All of her previous feelings about Stennett were gone, and in their place was a warm, thrilling sensation as she thought about the next time they'd be together.

She'd even forgotten for the moment why they were all there, and when she remembered, she started to worry.

When this party was over, which man was she going to leave with, Sawyer or Stennett?

As she closed her eyes and ran her palms over her sore nipples, she knew that she already had the answer to that.

Lenny Germaine dealt out another hand of poker, and Pete Bateman picked up his cards.

"You think this thing is gonna work?" Lenny asked.

"You've worked with Sawyer before," Bateman said. "You got any reason to think this won't work?"

"I don't know," Lenny said. "I've done a lot of things before, but I've never robbed a train."

"There's always a first time for everything," Bateman said.

"Yeah," Lenny said, "like a winning hand."

Bateman frowned and tossed his hand in while Lenny raked in the pot.

"Where did Stennett say he was going, anyway?" he asked, collecting the cards for another deal.

"He didn't."

"Didn't you ask him?"

"Why didn't you?"

"Me?" Bateman said. "He's your bodyguard, Count."

Lenny Germaine was about to answer when Stennett opened the door and entered.

"Well," Lenny said, "speak of the devil."

Stennett turned his eyes on Lenny and for a moment Lenny Germaine thought he might have said something wrong. Suddenly, to his and Bateman's surprise, Stennett smiled.

"Deal me in," he said. "I'm on a roll."

TWENTY-NINE

It was still an hour until his dinner with Forrest Evers when Clint got out of bed and started to dress.

"Where are you going?" Althea asked.

"I thought I'd walk around the train," he said. "Maybe get a drink from the bar."

"We can have a bottle of something brought in," she said. She was lying on her stomach, with her knees bent and her feet in the air. From that vantage point he had a perfect view of her perfect ass.

"We can't stay in here all afternoon," he said.

"Why not?"

"Because," he said, slapping her perfect rump, "I wouldn't survive it."

She smiled and rolled over, so he could see her breasts, and spread her legs so he could see . . . further.

"Are you sure?"

"Oh," he said, shaking his head, "I'm positive."

Clint went into the dining car and saw Ellie Lennox having a late lunch—or early dinner—alone.

"Mind if I join you?"

She looked up at him, frowning, then smiled.

"It won't blow your cover," he said softly.

141

"To hell with my cover," she said. "Sit down."

He sat.

"Want some lunch?" she asked. "Or is this dinner?"

"Whatever it is, I'll pass," he said. "I have a dinner appointment."

"Oh? Do I know her?"

"It's with the man who put this whole trip together," he said. "Evers."

"Oh."

"The man you're working for."

"Is that what I'm doing?" she asked. "Working?"

"Uh-oh. Somebody sounds unhappy."

"Maybe I should quit Pinkerton and go out on my own."

"Sure. Everybody's just waiting to hire a woman detective."

She made a face, then brightened.

"We could do it together."

"I'm not a detective."

"The hell you're not. You're the best detective I ever saw."

"Not the best I ever saw."

"No? Who's that?"

"Talbot Roper."

"Yep," she said. "That's the name I keep hearing whenever people talk about the best in the business. You know him, don't you?"

"I do."

"Think he wants a female partner? Or employee?"

"I don't know," Clint said. "I could ask him."

She gave him a quick look and said, "You could? Would you?"

"If that's what you really want."

"I just want to be able to do detective work, Clint. Not this throwaway stuff that Pinkerton doesn't want to use his best men—his best operatives—on."

"Give me the word and I'll drop in on Tal. I mean, we're going to be in Denver, right? Just think about it first."

She hesitated a moment, then said, "All right, I'll think about it."

He looked at his watch and decided to drop in on Evers early. They had some air to clear.

He stood up and said, "Where's your assistant, anyway?"

"I told him to go check out the sleeper and baggage cars."

"For what?"

"Who knows. I just got tired of doing everything myself."

He put his hand on her shoulder and said, "After this is over I'll buy you a big dinner in Denver."

"I'll hold you to that."

Five minutes after Clint left the dining car Al Wyatt came hurrying in.

"Lennox," he said.

"What are you rushing around for, Al?" she asked. "Sit down and have a cup of coffee."

"There's something you should see," he said.

"Where?"

"In the baggage car."

"Is it serious?"

"It's about as serious as it can get," he said, wiping his mouth with the back of his hand.

"All right," she said, rising, "lead the way."

• • •

When Evers let Clint into his cabin, the railroad man said, "Dinner won't be here for twenty minutes."

"That's fine with me," Clint said. "We've got some talking to do."

"About what?"

"About why you invited me along on this ride."

"Oh."

"Yeah, oh."

"I'm sorry."

"Why didn't you just tell me the truth?"

"That I wanted to hire you to use your reputation to scare away would-be robbers?"

"Yes."

"Would you have come?"

"No, and I would have told you how wrong you were."

"What do you mean?"

"My name isn't going to scare anyone away, Forrest. It'll be like honey to a fly."

"I don't understand."

"If somebody can rob this train while I'm on it and get away, that'll add to their reputation."

Evers thought about that for a moment then admitted, "I never looked at it that way."

"No, I guess you wouldn't have."

"Are you angry?"

"I guess I should be, but I'm not. I happen to be acquainted with some of the Pinkertons on this train," Clint said. "And if they need help, I'll be here to help them."

"I appreciate that."

"And I'd appreciate some straight answers, Forrest."

"Of course."

"Tell me about Althea."

"Althea? Why? What about her?"

"Why'd you hire her?"

"Because she was qualified."

"Who sent her to you?"

"No one."

"She just walked into your office and asked for a job?"

Forrest Evers thought a moment and then said, "Well, yes, I guess it happened that way."

"And how did she know you were looking for someone?"

"You know," he said, "I never asked her."

"Maybe you should have."

"What's this all about?"

"I guess I don't really know, Forrest," Clint said. "I'm just trying to justify some uncomfortable feelings I've been having."

"About what?" Evers asked, totally confused.

There was a knock at the door just then, which kept Clint from trying to answer that question.

When Evers opened it, Ellie Lennox stepped in, followed by Al Wyatt, who looked sick.

"Clint?"

"Who's this woman?"

"What's wrong, Ellie?"

"Mr. Wyatt?" Evers said, but Al Wyatt was too busy trying to keep his lunch down to answer.

"Al found something in the baggage car."

"What?" Clint asked.

"A body."

"A body?" Evers repeated. "Whose body? Who's been killed?"

Clint looked at Ellie Lennox and asked, "Do we know who he is, Ellie?"

"He had identification on him," she said, nodding. "His name was Samuel Grain."

THIRTY

The back of Sam Grain's head had been bashed in so severely that there was a lot of blood on the floor around him. No wonder Wyatt had looked so sick.

Clint bent over the body to examine it.

"Looks like one blow to the back of the head."

"With what?" Evers asked.

Clint shrugged.

"Some kind of heavy object. I can't tell what; I'm no coroner. When we get to Denver, the body can be properly examined."

"Denver?" Evers said. "There are places we can stop between here and Denver."

"If we do that," Clint said, "the killer could get off there, and we'd never catch him."

"What are you suggesting?" Ellie asked.

"That we keep this among the four of us." He looked at each of them in turn, Ellie, Evers and Al Wyatt. "If we pretend like we haven't discovered the body, the killer may get nervous and wonder why."

"But who would want to kill Sam Grain?" Evers asked.

"I can think of two people, off hand," Clint said.

"Who?" Ellie asked.

"I don't want to say yet, Ellie. Not until I've talked to them."

"Then what do we do with . . . with him?"

Sam Grain's body was lying in a small luggage berth, having been slipped in feet first and then covered. There had been so much blood, though, that Al Wyatt had accidentally stepped in it, slipping and almost falling.

"We can push his body farther in and cover it again, then clean up the blood."

"Who do you propose does that?" Evers asked, obviously worried that he would be asked to participate.

"You go back to your cabin, Forrest," Clint said. "See to your guests as if nothing had happened. The three of us will take care of . . . the body."

"You want me to act normal?" he asked, as if the request was out of the question. It was unusual, Clint knew, but certainly not out of the question.

"It's essential that you do, Forrest. If you can't, then have Althea see to them. Tell her that you're ill and must stay in your cabin."

"If I was ill she'd insist that I see a doctor."

Clint turned to look at him and asked, "Is there a doctor aboard?"

"Not one who works on the train, but we do have a guest—"

"No, I don't want any of the guests in on this. They're all suspects."

"What about railroad employees?" Ellie asked.

"Them, too," Clint said. "After all, Grain owned a piece of the railroad. They knew him."

"Sam never came down here," Evers said. "I dealt with the employees."

"Nevertheless, someone could have had a grudge

against him. We've got to keep this among us. Agreed?"

"Agreed," Ellie said. Al Wyatt didn't say anything, so Clint assumed that Ellie was speaking for him, and for Pinkerton's.

"Forrest?" Clint said. The man hesitated and Clint said, "You wanted me on this train, Forrest. Now that I'm here you'll have to do what I say."

"Yes, all right," Evers said. "I'll do what you say."

"Good. Go back to your room and stay there, as if you were having dinner. Get a hold of yourself, and then go out among your guests."

"All right . . . but will you tell me one thing?"

"What?"

"Who is this young lady?" he asked, pointing to Ellie.

After Forrest Evers had gotten his explanation and gone, Clint turned to Al Wyatt.

"Help me push him further in," he said, indicating Grain's body.

"You mean . . . touch it?" Wyatt said.

"Yes, you ninny!" Ellie said. "How the hell else would you move it except to touch it."

Wyatt looked at the body as if it would bite him.

"Come on, Al," Ellie said, "you've got no brains to add to this thing, at least use your muscles."

He gave her a quick look, then nodded to himself and helped Clint push Grain's body further into the baggage berth.

"We'll need some wet towels to clean up this blood," Clint said.

"I'll get them," Ellie said.

While she was gone, Clint and Wyatt found a tarpaulin and pushed it into the berth in front of the body, effectively hiding it from sight. When Ellie returned with soaking towels, they mopped up the blood as best they could, and hid the towels.

"Now what?" Ellie asked.

"We leave Al back here to guard the body," Clint said.

"Stay here?" Wyatt said. "With him? I mean, why guard it? Where's it going to go?"

Ellie gave him a look and was about to tear into him when he said, "All right, all right. I'll stay."

"Now, what was this you said about two suspects?" Ellie asked.

"Let's go somewhere where we can talk," Clint said. "I'll tell you what I know, and what I think I know."

THIRTY-ONE

"Are you involved with this Althea Saunders?" Ellie asked, but before Clint could answer she held up both of her hands. "No, don't answer that. It's none of my business. Let me get this straight," she said, and took a moment to formulate her thoughts.

"You're saying that either his partner, or his partner's secretary killed him?"

"Assistant."

"Assistant, secretary," Ellie said, waving away the difference. "She's a very attractive woman. Could she have been sleeping with one or both of them?"

"She could have been," Clint said. "I'll have to find that out."

"Does it—" she said, then stopped and shook her head to herself, telling herself to stop asking personal questions. She certainly had no claim on Clint Adams, and he didn't need to explain himself to her.

"All right, then find out," she said, "but tell me who you think killed him."

"I don't know," he said. "Evers said he was going to get rid of him one way or another."

"And Miss Saunders?"

"She hasn't said anything."

"Then what makes you suspect her?"

"It's just a feeling that something was going on be-tween them—and I don't necessarily mean something . . . sexual."

"What then?"

They were standing outside between cars, and Clint had had enough of yelling to be heard and straining to hear.

"Maybe I'd better go and find out," he said.

"I'll go back and make sure Al Wyatt is still con-scious," Ellie said. Shaking her head she added, "He may have fainted by now."

"When we're done with all of that, we'll have to find out if anyone saw Grain earlier this evening," Clint said, "but we'll have to do it without arousing anyone's suspicions about why we're asking."

"Wait a minute!" Ellie said, grabbing his arm. "Oh, am I dumb!" She struck herself in the forehead with the heel of her hand.

"What?"

"I saw him tonight!"

"You did?"

"I didn't know I did until just now," she said, think-ing back, "but now I'm sure it was him."

"What are you talking about?"

"Oh . . . damn!" she said, still reprimanding herself. "I was checking the train earlier, and when I walked into the second parlor car, he was walking out—and I could swear he was following someone."

"Following someone," Clint said, rubbing his jaw thoughtfully. "That sure doesn't sound like he was being forced to go against his will. That means that whoever he went with, he went willingly."

"Right."

"And who does a man go willingly to his death with?" Clint asked.

"A friend?"

"Or a woman," Clint added. "A good-looking woman—and there's no shortage of them on this train." There was only Althea, though, who had any connection with Grain that Clint knew of.

"If only I'd gone farther," she said.

"No use berating yourself now," Clint said. "Just go look after Wyatt, make sure he doesn't fall apart. I'll see you in a little while. There's a cocktail party in the parlor car before dinner."

"I'll be there."

They separated, Clint going into the sleeping car where Althea's cabin was, and Ellie back to the baggage car.

Ellie really didn't want to go back there again. It wasn't every day that she saw a body in that condition. In fact, she'd never seen a body in that condition before. Seeing how Wyatt had reacted, however, she was determined to put forward a stronger and braver face than he had.

She turned around, ran back out between the cars where she and Clint had been talking, and threw up.

THIRTY-TWO

Clint knocked on Althea's door, and when she answered him she knew something was wrong.

"What is it?"

"What is what?"

"You don't have that look on your face because everything's going fine," she said.

"What kind of a look is that?"

"Are we going to play games, Clint?"

"No," Clint said, entering the cabin, "no, Althea, we're not going to play games. We're going to talk very plainly and truthfully." He closed the door behind him.

"About what?" she asked. She was handsomely dressed in an eye-catching evening dress, apparently on her way to entertain the guests.

"About Sam Grain."

"What is there to talk about?" she asked. "He's Forrest's partner."

"And what is he to you?" Clint asked. When Althea didn't answer right away he said, "Or perhaps I should say, what *was* he to you?"

"Was?" she asked, frowning. "What do you mean was? What are you talking about?"

"What do you think I'm talking about?"

"I thought we weren't going to play any games, Clint," she said, an edge of desperation creeping into her voice. "Is he dead? Is that it?"

"He's in the baggage car with the back of his head stoved in."

"Dead?"

"As dead as they come."

She laughed aloud, clapped her hands together once and even did a little dance step. The sound of the clap was sharp and loud in the confined space of the small cabin.

"That's wonderful!"

Clint frowned.

"Somehow that's not the reaction I expected."

"Well, I hope you didn't expect me to shed tears for the bastard," Althea said. "Jesus, all the times I wanted to kill him and now somebody's done it."

It took him a few moments, but he finally found the word to describe her attitude.

She was relieved, and if she was acting, she was doing a damned good job of it.

"So you admit that you wanted to kill him."

"Sure I did . . ." she said, "but so did a lot of people."

"Like Forrest?"

She frowned, and then shook her head.

"Forrest wouldn't kill anyone."

She could have said, "Sure, Forrest killed him," and directed attention away from herself as a suspect, but she chose not to do that. Clint found that very interesting, as well.

"Do you want to ask me if I killed him?"

He nodded.

"Did you?"

"I didn't, but I wish I had."

"Why?"

"I'll give you the whole story in a nutshell," she said, and went on to explain about her "predicament."

"From then on he's treated me as if he owned me, putting his hands on me, forcing me to . . . to . . . Degrading me every chance he got . . ."

"Sexually?"

She hesitated, then nodded.

"And then he sent you to sleep with me."

She hesitated, then said, "Yes."

"Why?"

"He wanted to know why you were here, what you and Forrest were planning."

"Did he send you to apply for the job as Forrest's assistant?"

"He did."

"And you spied on Forrest for him."

"I did. I didn't want to go to jail."

"And that's the same reason you've been sleeping with me?"

"Yes—no! It's the reason I went with you that first day, and that first night. After that I slept with you because I wanted to, because you're the only man who's ever made me feel like . . . like some*one* instead of some*thing*. That means something to me, Clint."

"And you spied on me for him?"

"There wasn't anything to spy on you about," she said. "Don't you see? I could honestly tell Sam that you were just a guest of Forrest's."

"And he didn't believe you."

"No, so I could keep sleeping with you while making him think it was because he wanted me to. Don't you see? It was perfect."

"Nothing's perfect, Althea," he said. "I'll ask you again. Did you kill him?"

"Clint, if I wanted to kill him—if I ever had the nerve to do it—I've had plenty of opportunities. I wouldn't have had to wait until we were on this train."

"You would if you were counting on there being hundreds of suspects for the killing."

"But there aren't hundreds, are there?"

"No," he said, "as far as I'm concerned there are two who look just right for it."

"Me and Forrest."

"Right, and you just said Forrest Evers wouldn't kill anyone."

"He's incapable of it," she said, "and I didn't do it, so I suggest you look for another suspect."

"Sam Grain went to his death willingly, without realizing it. What would make him do that?"

"A woman," she said, without hesitating. "A beautiful woman he knew he could get to bed with."

"So a woman would just have to . . . flash her wares and he'd follow her?"

"Sam Grain was the most lecherous man I ever knew."

Clint noticed how easily she had slipped into the past tense.

"But I'm not the woman who led him down the garden path, Clint," she added. "You'll have to look elsewhere for that young lady."

"Young?"

"Young, old, as long as she was pretty and willing, Sam didn't care."

"Well, I'll be looking."

"Good. Let me know when you find her. Are we stopping anywhere along the way between here and

Denver to bring some law into this?" she asked.

"If we stop, the killer has a chance to get off. No, by the time we get to Denver, I'll have the killer all ready for the police."

"Do you want me to stay in my cabin?"

"No, there's no reason for that. You can continue to do your job."

"I won't have the job very much longer once you tell Forrest what I've been doing."

"Right now there's no reason to tell Forrest anything," Clint said, "and there's also no reason for you to tell anyone else about Sam Grain's death."

"I won't tell a soul."

"All right," he said, opening the door.

"Clint," she said, grabbing his arm, "about us—"

"We'll talk about that when this is all over, Althea."

She took her hand off his arm and said, "All right."

Clint left her cabin and closed the door behind him. His next stop would be Evers' cabin, for the same kind of "straight and honest" talk he'd just had with Althea.

THIRTY-THREE

Lola was looking out the window of her cabin when there was a knock on her door. Her stomach did a flip-flop as she wondered if it were Stennett coming back.

"Come in."

The door opened and Richard Sawyer walked in. He closed the door behind him and then took out his watch.

"We're getting close," he said. He was talking about the point where the five gunmen were waiting. "We're going to go out now and mingle with the guests. In half an hour we'll announce our intentions and start cleaning up. We should have everything well in hand by the time we reach our meeting point."

"Do you really think you can get them to stop the train?" she asked.

"Once we have these rich and famous guests under our guns, they'll do whatever we ask. Have you got your gun?"

"Yes," she said, picking up her purse. Inside of it was a small .22 caliber derringer.

"All right then, let's go."

She got up and moved toward the door.

161

"Are you all right?" he asked.

"Why do you ask?"

"You just don't look right."

"I'm fine, Rich," she said, "just fine."

"All right, then. Let's get it done."

"It's time," Lenny Germaine said to Bateman and Stennett. He assumed his "Count Germaine" accent and said, "Ve vill go and join ze others."

Bateman and Stennett rose and adjusted their gunbelts. Lenny had a .32 caliber revolver in a shoulder holster.

"Let's go," Stennett said. He was eager to get this over with. There were only two things he had on his mind.

The Gunsmith.

And Lola.

The cocktail party was going full tilt in the first parlor car. In the second car some of the even more rich and famous of the rich and famous were rubbing shoulders, drinking, smoking, and laughing.

Senator Creighton still had his young lady on his arm, although a half hour earlier she had been between his legs. He still felt the pleasant fatigue of trying to keep up with a girl her age, but prided himself that he was still able to do it. Back in Washington, his wife couldn't even keep up with *him*.

Mr. and Mrs. Judd were there, but she was at the far end of the car from her husband, stalking another young man since Clint Adams was nowhere in sight. This one was not quite as good-looking as Adams, but he had marvelous shoulders and was supposed to be a prizefighter of some sort.

Robert Louis Stevenson was standing alone, his mind still on what he had been writing back in his room. He was also scanning the car for any sign of Clint Adams. He found the man fascinating.

Count Germaine and his bodyguards were listening to the mindless prattle of the famous actress, while Richard Sawyer and Lola were doing much of the same with the famous actor. The actor and actress would occasionally throw each other a murderous glance across the car.

Althea Saunders was standing with someone who was talking to her, but to whom she was paying no heed. She was thinking about Sam Grain and Clint Adams. The man she had wanted so long to be rid of was gone, and the man she wanted to hold onto was almost gone.

She had to figure out a way to keep him.

"So when you talked about different ways of getting rid of him, you never meant killing him."

"No, of course not," Forrest Evers said. "I didn't like Sam, Clint, but I didn't hate him—not enough to kill him, anyway. You've got to believe me."

Evers had been in a sweat ever since Clint had entered his cabin and begun questioning. Still, he continued to dress for his cocktail party.

"I'd like to, Forrest," Clint said, "I really would."

"Look," Evers said, pulling on his jacket, "I've got to get outside. Althea can't handle both cars at once."

"You've decided you can handle it, then? Go out there and act like nothing's happened?"

"My stomach is churning, Clint. First Sam is found dead, and then you accuse me of killing him. I'm not in the best frame of mind, but I've got responsibilities

to take care of. For Christ's sake, you don't think I'm
going to jump off my own train, do you?"

"No, Forrest, I don't think that. Come on, we'll
both go out to the party."

"Maybe somebody will say or do something to give
themselves away?" Forrest said hopefully.

"Somebody will," Clint said. "By the time we get
to Denver, somebody will."

THIRTY-FOUR

When Clint and Althea joined the party in the second car, Ellie was already working the party in the first car. She was drawing looks from people, and she knew it was because of the way she was dressed, but she hadn't brought a change of clothes with her. She hadn't anticipated that she would be attending any of the fancy parties that would be thrown. That was to be Al Wyatt's function.

When she had checked on Wyatt after leaving Clint, she had found him sitting on someone's trunk, looking very pale and drawn.

"Al, how did someone as big and strong as you turn out to be such a—" she started, and then stopped. Under normal circumstances she didn't like him, but ever since being saddled with him she'd been snapping at him left and right. She decided to give it a break.

"I'm sorry—"

"Don't apologize, Ellie," he said, looking at his huge hands. "I guess I'm just not cut out to be a Pinkerton. I'll resign when we get back."

"Don't do that on my account. I'm not going to try to blame this on you."

"I know you won't—"

"Look," she said, suddenly feeling compassion for him, "if we solve this murder, you won't have to quit. We'll both get a raise."

"Do you think so?"

He looked up at her, and she noticed for the first time that he was an extremely attractive man. If only he had been more like Clint . . .

"We'll see," she said, patting his hand. "I'm sorry you have to stay back here. If we had someone else—"

"It's all right," he said. "You go and find the murderer. I'll do my part."

She'd smiled at him and left the baggage car . . .

. . . Now she was circulating through the party, listening in on conversations, and drawing those looks because she wasn't dressed as fancy as everyone else. The women especially were casting disapproving looks her way. The men, despite the way she was dressed, couldn't help noticing how attractive she was, but she was able to separate and identify those looks.

She decided to go and look for Clint in the other car. He knew more of the people involved than she did. If she had to bet money, she'd bet that Clint was going to be the one to solve this thing.

As Clint and Althea entered the second car, Althea left his side and went over to Forrest. He watched as they spoke to each other in a hushed tone, probably about Sam Grain's murder. Clint couldn't help but wonder *how* they were talking about it. As two people who knew him and were sorry or glad he was dead? Or as two people who had planned and executed his death perfectly?

Maybe they were getting their stories straight?

He walked over to them, and as he had expected, they stopped talking.

Richard Sawyer was standing at one end of the second car with Lola, while "Count Germaine" and his bodyguards were at the other end.

Lenny Germaine, Pete Bateman, and Tom Stennett were all supposed to have their eyes on Sawyer, waiting for the signal to move.

Finally, Sawyer gave it.

Stennett, usually the consummate professional, almost missed the signal because his eyes were riveted to the Gunsmith. It was as if he were a starving man and Clint Adams was an available meal.

Finally, the chance to really face somebody with a bigger rep than he had. Hickok was gone, and in his wake other legends grew larger. One of the largest was that of the Gunsmith.

And after this, one of the largest would be that of Tom Stennett.

Finally, he looked at Sawyer just in time to catch the signal.

Clint saw what was happening a split second too late to be able to do anything about it.

"Forrest—" he said, grabbing Evers' arm. The man looked at him inquiringly, but the guns were already out and one of the men was trying to get everyone's attention. Clint couldn't draw his gun because there were too many people between him and the gunmen. He was going to have to bide his time.

"Clint?" Forrest Evers said.

"Don't do anything," Clint said urgently to both Evers and Althea, who were puzzled. "Just follow my lead."

"Your lead?" Evers said. "But what—"

That was all Evers was able to get out when he was silenced by the shot.

Sawyer gave the signal and pulled his gun. Lola drew hers from her purse. At the other end of the car Germaine, Bateman, and Stennett all followed suit.

"Excuse me," Sawyer shouted, "ladies and gentlemen, excuse me, please."

When no one paid him any mind he looked across the room at Stennett and nodded.

Tom Stennett fired his gun once, the bullet harmlessly striking one of the hanging chandeliers without damaging any of the lamps. It did, however, succeed in gaining everyone's attention.

Clint looked across the car at the man who fired the shot and recognized him, mentally kicking himself for not having done so before.

Tom Stennett!

"Ladies and gentlemen," Richard Sawyer said, "this is a stickup."

THIRTY-FIVE

"Now," Sawyer said, "if everyone will just listen carefully, we can avoid the unpleasantness of anyone getting hurt."

"Sawyer," Evers said, "what the hell—" but he stopped when Sawyer turned and pointed his gun at him.

"Mr. Evers, I realize that I am your invited guest, and as such my behavior might be described as boorish—but shut the hell up!"

At that point the far door to the car suddenly opened, and Ellie Lennox stepped in.

"Hi, sweetheart," Pete Bateman said, grabbing her arm and pulling her to him. "Join the party."

Sawyer gave Lenny Germaine a look and Lenny moved to the door and locked it. Anyone wanting to get in would have to knock, thereby announcing themselves.

Now Sawyer turned to face his captive audience once again.

"Now, as you can all see there are five of us here, all armed, more than enough for the job we have at hand."

"Which is?" Evers asked.

Sawyer whirled on him, then relaxed, and said, "All right, that's a fair question. We intend to rob everyone present of their money and valuables."

"You can't be serious—" someone said, but before Sawyer could turn, Stennett had already whipped his gun around, smacking the speaker across the jaw with it.

"I would urge all of you to do as you are told and speak only when you are spoken to. That tall, slender gentleman over there has a very short temper."

"Look," said Senator Creighton, making a show of courage for his young blonde girlfriend, "there are only five of them, and they're here to rob us, not kill us. We can't allow them to just rob us."

"Mister, I'd recommend that you shut up," Lola said.

"I beg your pardon, young lady, but I have every right to speak—"

"Honey—" the blonde on his arm said warningly, but he patted her hand.

"Don't worry dear. These people are cowards. They wouldn't dare shoot any of us. What about the rest of you!" he spoke up. "Are you with me?"

There was a murmur from some of the men, but before it could become a vote of support, Stennett stepped forward and shot Senator Creighton in the heart. The Senator did not even have time to gasp, he just fell to the floor, dead.

"Don't start screaming, honey," Lola said to the girl, "or you'll be next."

The girl simply gaped at the Senator's body and put both hands over her mouth.

"Jesus Christ!" Forrest Evers yelled. "That was a United States Senator!"

"*Was* is the operative word, Mr. Evers," Sawyer said.

"Can't you control him?" Evers asked, pointing at Stennett.

"In a word," Sawyer said, "no—and that's exactly why I brought him. Do you understand, Evers?"

Evers started to speak, but Clint grabbed his arm to silence him, and at the same time made a very interesting discovery.

"He understands," Clint said.

"Ah, the famous Gunsmith speaks," Richard Sawyer said. "Have you any intention of trying to stop us, Mr. Gunsmith?"

"None," Clint said tightly.

"Because Mr. Stennett over there would like nothing better."

"I'm sure of that."

"All right, then," Sawyer said, "now that everybody knows their places, here's what we're going to do."

Lola made a round of the room, collecting all money and jewelry in a canvas sack, one of several that Sawyer had packed their luggage with.

After that, Sawyer announced that one by one people would be taken to their cabin by one of the men, where they would produce any valuables that they had there.

"Afterward, we'll go on to the next car and do the same."

"You don't have enough men," Clint said.

"What?" Sawyer asked.

"You don't have enough men to have someone go into the next car. There are more people in there then in here."

"I know that," Sawyer said. "The very rich are in

here, and the merely rich are in there."

"But you don't have enough men—"

"Don't worry about that," Sawyer said, checking his watch. "In a very short time I'll have all the men I need. We'll be making an unscheduled stop, Mr. Evers, and you will be giving the order for the train to stop."

That information was what Clint was after. Something had to be done fairly quickly before they made an unscheduled stop to take on more thieves.

"I won't—"

"He'll cooperate," Clint assured Sawyer.

"Good. That's all we really want, here, is a little cooperation."

While the collections were finishing up Evers leaned over and whispered to Clint, "I have—"

"I know," Clint said. "Quiet."

Evers had been going to tell Clint that he had his sleeve gun on, but Clint already knew that. He'd felt it when he grabbed Evers' arm.

"Somebody's missing," Lola said, suddenly.

"What?" Sawyer said. "Who?"

"That old geezer and his chubby wife."

Clint realized that she was talking about the Judds. Now that she had mentioned it, Clint realized that sometime during the party they had gone. Into the next car, or to their cabin?

"We'll check their cabin," Sawyer said. "If they're not there they're in the next car."

Lola nodded and continued making her collection.

Across the room Bateman had released Ellie, but she was still standing near him. She looked at Clint, who hoped that she wouldn't move until he did.

When Lola reached Ellie with her canvas bag, Ellie hesitated.

"The purse, sweetie," Bateman said, grabbing the drawstring purse that Ellie was holding. Clint flinched, because if there was a gun in that bag, its weight would give it away, and then Ellie would have some explaining to do. Luckily, there was apparently no gun. Clint hoped that she had one on her, somewhere.

"All right," Sawyer said when the collections were over. "Everybody move against the wall."

Everyone moved as instructed and soon one wall was lined with people. Clint was down at one end with Evers and Althea, while Ellie was at the other.

"One by one we will be taking you to your cabin, but that won't be for several minutes yet. Mr. Evers?"

"Yes?"

"It's just about time to stop the train."

"Argue," Clint whispered, hoping that Evers heard him.

There was a moment's pause and then Forrest Evers finally said, "I won't."

"What?" Sawyer asked.

"I will not."

"I thought we were past this," Sawyer said, his tone one of exasperation.

"You can't scare me," Evers said.

"Why is that?"

"You need me to stop the train, so you can't kill me."

"But if you refuse to stop the train," Sawyer said, "I might as well kill you."

"Forrest, for Christ's sake, do what the man says and stop the train," Clint said.

"I will not!" Evers told Clint.

Clint grabbed Evers by the arm and turned him around. As he did so he triggered the sleeve mechanism that held the gun and the derringer slid into his hand.

He knew he had to take Stennett out first, and with the derringer it would have to be a head shot. Next he'd have to shoot Sawyer, and then he'd be out of bullets.

Jesus, he hoped Ellie had a gun somewhere!

THIRTY-SIX

"Mrs. Judd," Al Wyatt said nervously.

"Heather," Heather Judd said to him. "Sweet Al, you can call me by my first name. After all, I *am* about to suck your—oh, my God, it's so big!"

Al Wyatt nervously thought about Sam Grain's body, which was about three feet away from Heather Judd as she knelt on the floor in front of him and pulled out his rigid penis. Even the thought of the dead body couldn't keep him from sporting a raging erection, especially since Mrs. Judd had removed her dress and was naked—and *her* body was about as alive as a body can get! She had incredibly large breasts, and now she was rolling his penis between them, flicking her tongue out and licking the swollen head.

Al hoped Ellie wouldn't come walking in at that moment. He knew his behavior was unprofessional, but Jesus, he couldn't just tell Mrs. Judd no when she came into the car and announced that she'd been looking all over for him and now that she had found him she intended to—not *wanted* to, but *intended* to—have sex with him.

Could he?

* * *

Clint pushed Forrest Evers away from him, saying, "You stupid fool—" and while everyone was watching Evers fall, he shot Tom Stennett through the right eye with the derringer.

"Jesus!" Sawyer said, turning toward Clint, but already he was too late. Sawyer put his hand up, but the little slug went through it and struck him in the throat.

When Clint shot Stennett, Ellie moved quickly. She stomped on Pete Bateman's instep, then pulled her skirt up and pulled out a Colt .32 revolver. She shot Bateman in the chest, then turned and saw the blonde woman pointing her gun at Clint.

She and the woman fired at the same time.

The slug hit Clint high up on the right side, in the chest, almost in the shoulder. As he staggered back a step he saw Ellie's shot bloody the woman's blonde hair as a chunk of flesh flew off the top of her head.

There was another shot then, which he couldn't locate. He tensed for the impact of another slug.

Al Wyatt had Heather Judd's big breasts in his hands, lifting them to his mouth, and she had her hands wrapped around his penis, which was aching to burst. Al wanted to drive himself into her, but he also wanted to suck her breasts. He didn't exactly know which to do first, so he was all thumbs, and Mrs. Judd was beginning to lose interest. Even though she'd found a man with a huge penis, he didn't seem to know what to do with it. That was the reason she had been looking over his head—wishing she'd been able to isolate Clint Adams instead of this inept lover—in time to see her husband coming up behind Al Wyatt with a metal bar.

"Winnie!" she cried out. "No, not again!"

Al Wyatt reacted violenly. He pushed Mr. Judd away from him, ducked the metal bar Winston Judd was swinging at him, and hit Judd on the point of the jaw with his big fist. The man dropped like he'd been shot.

"What the hell—" Wyatt said.

Mrs. Judd sighed and said, "He's so jealous." She turned vacant eyes on Al Wyatt and said, "He'll kill any man who touches me. Isn't that sweet?"

Ellie heard the other shot and whirled around in time to see Lenny Germaine fall to the floor, clutching his stomach. A man was standing over him, holding a gun. Ellie looked at Pete Bateman's body and saw that his gun was gone, apparently in the hand of the man who had just fired.

The man turned to her and smiled.

"Dave Simmons," he said. "Pinkerton's."

She'd identified him as Bull Gifford, the boxer.

"What the hell happened here!" Al Wyatt shouted aloud.

Everyone in the parlor car looked at him and stared. He had Winston Judd slung over his shoulder, and a half-dressed Heather Judd hanging on his arm, her breasts exposed.

Wyatt looked curiously at the bodies that seemed to have been strewn haphazardly about, and then at

Clint Adams, who was bleeding from the shoulder. He had Althea Saunders and Ellie Lennox administering to his wound.

"They tried to rob the train, Al," Ellie explained. "Clint and I and Dave Simmons here—who's a Pinkerton, not a boxer—stopped them."

"While I was sitting in the baggage car?" Wyatt said. Almost negligently, he allowed Winston Judd to slide from his shoulder to the floor. His wife sat down, lifted his head and placed it in her lap.

"Sweet man," she said. "He's so jealous."

"What happened to them?" Clint asked.

"This man tried to brain me with an iron bar!" Wyatt said, pointing down at Judd.

"Why?" Ellie asked, looking at Heather Judd's fat breasts. None of the men in the room thought they were fat, though. Most of them thought they were just fine, and in the wake of the violence that had just erupted, appreciated having something to take their minds off of it.

"Well, I, uh, she was—that is, we were—"

"We get the picture, Al," Ellie said, applying the last piece of tape to Clint's bandage. He stood up and slid his shirt back on.

"Thank you, ladies," he said to Althea and Ellie, who exchanged appraising glances.

Everyone seemed to have forgotten that there were five dead men and a dead woman on the floor—including Senator Creighton.

Forrest Evers stared at Heather Judd's breasts and said, "What the hell else is going to happen?"

"Nothing else, Forrest," Clint said. "We've stopped the robbery, and Al Wyatt of Pinkerton's has found our killer."

"I did?"

"He has?" Evers asked.

Wyatt recovered nicely and said, "Well, of course I did. It was obvious."

Ellie looked at Clint and said, "Obvious."

"Ladies and gentlemen," Clint said to the people assembled, "I'm afraid we're going to need some help cleaning up here."

THIRTY-SEVEN

"I can't believe it," Forrest Evers said. "A jealous husband."

"A crazy husband," Althea added.

"With a crazy wife," Clint said.

They were all three seated at a table in the dining room of the Denver House Hotel. Clint was staying there and although both Evers and Althea had stayed the previous night, they were headed back to Chicago.

"Who would ever have thought it to look at them?" Evers said.

"A lot of crazy people look normal, Forrest," Clint said.

"Yeah," Evers said. "Look at me."

"What do you mean?" Althea asked.

"I look normal, don't I?"

"Of course."

"Well, that train ride has made me crazy. I mean, a dead United States senator, for Christ's sake. And that's not the worst thing! I mean, he wasn't a very good senator, anyway, but . . . Christ! How am I going to survive this?"

"Just explain things," Clint said. "I'm sure people will understand. After all, we did manage to save

181

everyone from being robbed."

"And a murderer was caught," Althea said.

"All by the Pinkertons," Clint added. "I mean, everyone should be happy. You supplied just the right amount of security."

"Clint, you can't be serious," Althea said. "If it wasn't for you, none of that—"

"I started things off with Forrest's gun, Althea," Clint said, interrupting her. "It was the two Pinkertons who did the rest—and Ellie Lennox saved my life."

"I'm sure you're indebted to her for that," Althea said.

"And it was a Pinkerton who caught Sam Grain's killer."

"That was only because Heather Judd couldn't get to you, so she went after the first pair of pants she found free."

"He still caught the killer," Clint said. "You can't take that away from him."

"Still, you should take some credit." Althea said.

"I don't want any credit," Clint said. "Let Old Allan and his people have it all."

"Well," Forrest said, "we'd better be going if we want to catch our train."

"I'll be along in a minute," Althea said.

Evers nodded and left the dining room.

"I want to thank you for not telling Forrest about . . . Sam and me."

"I expect you to do that."

"I will," she said. "During the ride back, I'll tell him all of it."

"Good girl."

"Of course," she said, "I could leave tomorrow—"

Clint shook his head and Althea stopped.

"Is it that lady detective?" she asked.

"She's a friend," Clint said, "just as you are."

"*Just* as I have been?" Althea said. "Never mind, don't answer that."

She stood up and Clint stood with her. Ignoring the looks of the people around them she gave him a long, lingering kiss, caressing the back of his neck.

"Come to Chicago once in a while, hmm?"

"I'll visit," he said, "sometime."

"Yeah," she said, sliding her hand down his chest, "sure. 'Bye."

"Good-bye, Althea."

Clint turned to look for the waiter to settle up the check and found himself facing the disapproving glare of the head waiter.

"Can I help you?" he asked.

"Yes, sir, you may—by keeping *that* sort of behavior in your room."

"In my room?"

"Yes, sir."

"My good man," he said, handing him the money for the check and thinking of Ellie Lennox waiting for him in his room, "that is just what I am going to do."

Watch for

WHEN LEGENDS DIE

eightieth novel in the exciting
GUNSMITH series

coming in August!

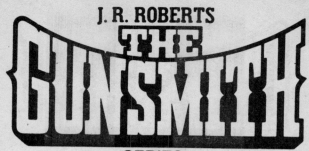

J. R. ROBERTS
THE GUNSMITH
SERIES

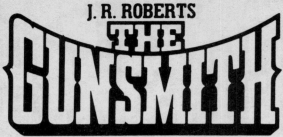

J. R. ROBERTS
THE GUNSMITH
SERIES